GW00480522

ENTERTAINMENT TECHNOLOGY PRESS

Biographical Series

*To Jackie, John and Ken at ETP who have patiently converted
my scribbles into ten books*

A THEATRIC MISCELLANY

Francis Reid

To cleveland

with best wishes

[signature]

PROBABLY MY LAST BOOK
BUT NEVER - SAY - NEVER !

etpress

Entertainment Technology Press

A Theatric Miscellany

© Francis Reid

First published September 2015
Entertainment Technology Press Ltd
The Studio, High Green, Great Shelford, Cambridge CB22 5EG
Internet: www.etnow.com

ISBN 978 1 904031 87 1

A title within the
Entertainment Technology Press Biographical Series
Series editor: John Offord

CONTENTS

A THEATRIC MISCELLANY

I never expected to be alive in 2015 but, aided by five daily pills, I have reached 84 and there are no immediate signs of an early demise. Having survived dropsy, open heart surgery and a perforated gall bladder during my early eighties, my health is now stable. I have learned to live with a catheterised bladder and gout distorted fingers. A wobbly balance restricts my mobility: I can move around the house unaided but outside I need a Zimmer frame or wheeled rollator. I have a hunch that my balance may be something of a mindset problem but that does not make it less real.

The deterioration of Jo's hearing and sight makes me realise how lucky I am that my eyes and ears still function although my optician has referred me for cataract surgery. Eating and drinking remain a pleasure. I miss my once regular travelling to European Opera Houses but have wonderful memories. I am grateful to be living in the age of the DVD.

The only certainty in life is death. At my age its timing leans towards sooner rather than later. However, it seems a long way from being imminent. I have no fear of death, except perhaps the manner of it, and no expectation of an afterlife. But never-say-never. The real consequence of death is that what happens next for my family and in world history will remain a mystery.

This book is about memories. Some of them are highlights of my life. Recall of other, more routine events, is triggered by discovery of a cache of sundry articles. A few make predictions that are still relevant but most guess the future wrongly. Either way, they make a small contribution to history.

1 MEMORIES

Remembered Remarks

As memory details fade, it is often remarks – heard or overheard – that remain. These remarks may have pained, pleasured or stimulated.

When lighting was interrupted for a lunch break, Douglas Craig inadvertently exclaimed: "Isn't it wonderful the way it all comes to life under working light!" The profuseness of his apologies did little to alleviate the pain which I tried to hide with rather forced laughter. Freddie Carpenter's "Well, Francis, I have a set designed in the most exquisitely delicate shades of lavender and you flood it with brothel pink light," did nothing for my confidence at the beginning of a lighting career.

My lighting of the London production of *Bubbling Brown Sugar* in the absence of the Broadway director raised polite approval from the set designer with the caveat "but will Cooper like it". The theatre was in a state of apprehension on the day of his arrival. "Cooper has landed". "Cooper is in a Limo". "Cooper has checked-in". "Cooper's at breakfast". "Cooper is on his way to the theatre". "Cooper is at the stage door". And in walked a pleasant, rather charming, little man. We ran through the complex opening sequence. "Fine," he says, "but too much too soon." The next scene was judged "Fine, but too little too late." And then "That's it. That's what I always wanted and never got." (All I had done was to use parcans in strong colours whereas New York had given it McCandless tints.)

Some remarks, such as Carl Ebert's "Can you hear the light?" uttered on a change of key, tempo or phrase, were helpfully constructive. A chance encounter with Sir Michael Redgrave in a corridor during early rehearsals of *La Boheme* at Glyndeboume provided the key to the lighting style. "By the way," Francis, "I am sure that we are remembering, are we not, that gaslight is green." "Yes, Michael," I replied although this was news to me. Experiment with a touch of green in the gel mix showed how right he was. A sufficiently pale green was achieved by bleaching Cinemoid 38 in the sun for eight hours. Hearing this story, Michael Hall arranged for Rosco to produce a gaslight green filter.

Other remarks can be particularly unhelpful. Shown a lit scene, Keith Hack directing Tennessee Williams' *Vieux Carre* at the Piccadilly responded: "No, that's not it." "Intensity? Contrast? Colour?" I enquired and the response was: "I don't know – show me something else and I'll let you know." But even such experiences can have their reward. In the bar on the first night, after particularly unhappy rehearsals, Tennessee said: "Hey Francis, lights are looking good tonight." Overhearing this, Keith responded with: "No they're not, they're a load of crap." Who did I choose to believe?

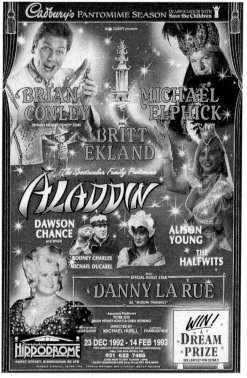

Pantomime with Michael Hurll

Michael Hurl, after watching the first few cues of a panto lighting rehearsal said "Can I go home now? I like what I see and you are motoring!" During rehearsals we developed silent remarks with a hand gesture language for up, down, open out, close in, crossfade, and rebalance which I subsequently used in all rehearsal rooms to avoid disturbing actor concentration.

"I wish you lighting design chaps had been invented years ago," said Hilton Edwards, a director renowned for his lighting expertise, as we made the final adjustments on the morning of the premiére of his production of Brian Friel's *Philadelphia, Here I Come!*

But the ultimate compliment came from Anton Rodgers. After he had given copious notes to the cast of *Flashpoint* I enquired if he had anything for me. Flicking over the pages of his spiral notebook he replied: "I'm sorry. I didn't notice the lighting tonight."

Remembering Britten on the occasion of his Centenary (2013)

Wagner, Verdi and Britten on stage, television, radio, DVD and CD. There is a plethora of exhibitions, books and conferences. The anniversary industry is in full flood with performances. Reminiscences abound, although in the case of the Verdi and Wagner bicentenaries, they are inevitably second hand. The Britten centenary, however, is able to draw upon the memories of many people who knew or worked with the composer.

In 1957, with but a couple of backstage years under my belt, I found myself in Aldeburgh stage managing for the English Opera Group. Aldeburgh's Opera House – the Jubilee Hall – was then rather more primitive than it is now. Everything – boards, bars, booms and braces – had to be brought up from London with the sets. These were the days when everything had to be taken to Liverpool Street Station, loaded into trucks and attached to a train for Aldeburgh where there was no shunting engine so the trucks were eased into the loading bay by pushing a metal shoe on a long pole under a wheel. In addition to the usual running of rehearsals and performances, the stage management trio, augmented by Bill Ewer, a truly wonderful local carpenter, provided the crew for getting-in, fitting-up, scene-changing, board operating and getting-out. This was top quality international opera on a village hall scale.

Ben was everywhere, quietly but firmly ensuring the highest of standards. It was a thrilling time to be alive and working in such an ensemble.

Albert Herring had its final performance with the original cast in John Piper's Glyndebourne scenery and there was a production of Lennox Berkely's *Ruth*. Of this opera I have

Joan Cross as Lady Billows in Albert Herring

little recall but I do remember that on the first night, when a lamp on the spot bar blew after 'beginners', I climbed the ladder in my kilt while the chorus trilled: "Now we know"! The team also stage managed concerts in the Jubilee Hall and the Parish Church.

In the autumn, we took the original *Turn of the Screw* production to the Berlin Festival for its final revival and I made an operatic gaffe that is imprinted on my memory. After the first night, composer, cast, orchestra and crew descended into the bierkeller at the stage door for sausages and sauerkraut. When the conversation turned to tempi variations from one performance to another, Ben suggested that the problem did not arise when composers conducted their own works. I chipped in with the information that the timings for all the performances of *The Turn of the Screw* were logged in the prompt score and there was a variation of plus or minus several minutes. The resultant deathly hush was broken by Peter Pears who rescued me with: "Yes, Ben, Francis is right – sometimes I have a problem keeping up with you while at other times I have barely enough breath to finish a phrase." Other singers agreed with enthusiasm and someone, probably Colin Graham, pointed out that it was part of the magic of live performance that artists responded to many factors, particularly audience response.

Much relieved and considerably wiser, I survived to be hired for the 1958 Season, becoming technical director. The big production of that season was the premiére of *Noye's Fludde* in Orford Church. Coordinating the singers, animals and orchestra from several schools, professional orchestral players, bugle and handbell teams was quite a logistic exercise. But when we brought everyone together for the first time, and it all fell smoothly into place, was a magic moment rarely repeated and never on any west end musical that I subsequently worked on.

Perhaps the trickiest task was ensuring that no copy of the vinyl recording made by Ben, Peter and Imgoen Holst to help teachers prepare their animals, strings and recorders, fell into the hands of LWT television who were filling their

Noyes Fludde premiere in Orford Church

Sunday evening god slot with a live transmission. Ben was adamant that the work should speak for itself without the kind of introduction that a TV executive had been overheard to suggest as 'Ludo Kennedy on a tombstone'.

The composer insisted that it was to be played under full-up white light although Colin and I eventually talked him into a 50% dim during the storm. A rig of pageants (beamlights with parabolic reflectors and spill rings) was planned but Strand had just got around (at last!) to Fresnels and we used prototypes of the Pattern 143.

And in the same season – the stuff that Festivals are made of – a double bill for two performances only of *Les Mamelles de Tiresias* and *Il Ballo dell Ingrate* directed by John Cranko in designs by Osbert Lancaster and John Piper. Alas, last-minute illness prevented Poulenc's participation in Britten's two piano arrangement for Apollinaire's sex change opera bouffe. The centre-parted wavy

Osbert Lancaster's designs for Poulenc's Les Mamelles de Tirésias

lacquered wig and outrageously drooping moustache of Peter Pears in drag and the balloon bosom of Jennifer Vyvyan taking flight are images to be cherished.

Today we are in Aldeburgh for the opening of *The Cominge of the Fludde* exhibition marking the 50th anniversary of Benjamin Britten's *Noye's Fludde*. As stage director (the then title for stage manager) of the English Opera Group, I was deeply involved in the premiére while Jo, in an advanced state of pregnancy in expectation of Angus, sat in on rehearsals and lent a hand from time to time in the wardrobe. So, for both of us, the display of designs, masks, photos and other ephemera is an instant transportation back to a time when we had just celebrated our first wedding anniversary. The exhibition at The Red House where Ben wrote the opera and an overnight in the White Lion after a gentle stroll along Crag Path past the Jubilee Hall to sit on the sea wall for fish and chips makes for just the kind of all our yesterday's experience that is a joy of growing old.

The first time I heard Vivaldi's *Seasons* was at the Aldeburgh Festival of 1958. The soloist was Yehudi Menuhin, Benjamin Britten conducted from the harpsichord and I was in the prompt comer. In place of the Italian sonnets (poet unknown but possibly Vivaldi himself) written to accompany this early example of programme music, the four concerti were interspersed with readings by Peter Pears of extracts from George Thompson's poem *The Seasons* which formed the basis of the libretto for Haydn's oratorio on the subject.

Highlights particularly remembered
as a lighting designer

- Mirella Freni as Elvira in Bellini's *I Puritani* at the Wexford Festival
- Keith Michelle in *Man of la Mancha* at the Picadilly Theatre
- Jacques Brel in *L'homme de la Mancha* at Theatre des Champs Elysees
- *Bubbling Brown Sugar* in London, Brussels and Paris

Bubbling Brown Sugar

- *Sleuth* at St Martins Theatre and Michodiere Paris (*Jeu, set et Match*)
- *Anyone for Dennis?* at Whitehall Theatre
- Malcolm Williamson's *The Growing Castle* at Dynevor Castle and Gothenburg.
- *Teseo* at Teatro Rinnuovati in Siena
- *Siroe* at RCM Britten Theatre for London Handel Festival
- David Mamet's *A life in The Theatre* at Open Space Theatre in London

Sleuth programme

Handel's Siroe at London Handel Festival

as a stage manager

- *Noyes Fludde* in Orford Church
- *A Wish for Jamie* in Glasgow Alhambra
- *Albert Herring* in Aldeburgh Jubilee Hall

Prophets of doom confounded by Bury Royal success

For a long time the doom-mongers have been shaking their heads sadly and sagely over the Theatre Royal at Bury St. Edmunds.

Not viable, they intone, not large enough; it's bound to fail.

True, it had gone through a lean and difficult time up to the end of last summer. But now the picture looks warmly different — and after his first six months as administrator, Francis Reid can say with that beaming, imperturbable confidence which is his trademark: "We're in the black now."

VARIETY

Between September and Christmas, he points out, they averaged 70 per cent of their 350-seat capacity. Towards the end of the year "A Christmas Carol" pulled in the audiences to mark up a 90 per cent box office "take."

For the full autumn season, some 19,000 seats were booked, with perhaps a wider repertoire of product on display than this enchanting little Georgian theatre has seen in modern times.

Variety, in fact, is Francis Reid's campaign policy — "Something for everybody" is the catchline. And it seems to be working. Even in the distinctly different entertainment offered last week — and soon to be seen in Norwich when Premises fix a date — when Incubus Theatre presented their vulgar Roman pastiche, "The Golden Ass."

"I really have tried to broaden the repertoire here," he says. "It seemed to me that previously it was a theatre *in* Bury rather than *for* Bury. This is what we have to change."

as a theatre manager

- eliminating deficit and raising profile of Theatre Royal Bury St Edmunds (1979)

as a member of the audience

- Handel Festivals in Gottingen, Halle, Karlsruhe and London (pictured below)
- Handel operas in dozens of German city theatres

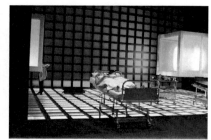

Gottingen Handel Festival

Admeto at Halle Handel Festival

Some Travel Memories

Elephants caparisoned for a Pooram

- Elephant Pooram in Kerala, India
- Standing on the bare stage of the Bolshoi Theatre
- Landing at the old Kai Tak airport in Hong Kong

On the stage of the Bolshoi

Continental Lighting (1961) – from *The Stage*

Needing a replacement for their 1934 Bordoni transform lighting control, Glyndebourne Opera sent me on a three-week study tour of 20 different theatres in 15 German, Austrian and Belgian towns.

Like every other technical aspect of the Continental theatre, the lighting installation and organisation is planned for a daily repertory programme change rather than for a long run of one production. Thus the first requirement of lighting layout is accessibility. When spots have to be reset daily for the performance and frequently twice-daily if there is a morning rehearsal, there is obviously little point in thinking in terms of climbing a stepladder to a spotbar.

The main lighting is therefore carried on bridges and towers: every theatre has an adjustable false proscenium which can vary the width and height of the opening. Built into this, so that they move with the proscenium, are the main bridge and vertical perch towers. The bridge is normally in two levels and carries an assortment of soft-edge and profile lanterns.

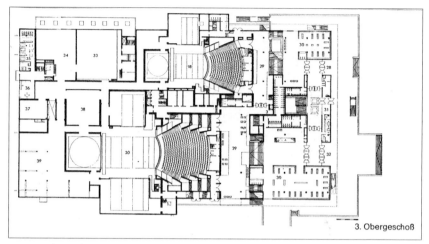

3. Obergeschoß

Wurzburg Staatstheater showing typical civic opera house and playhouse configuration

Equipment for scene projection is also carried, since the grids are so high that it is possible not only to light far upstage but to project on to the cyclorama. The majority of spots are simple focus spots with plano-convex lens systems and, while Fresnel lenses are likely to be adopted in greater numbers, the use of more complex mirror systems is likely to be confined to special effects, as the stages are so large that they do not have our problems of restricting lantern beams to a hard edge in order to keep clear of scenery.

Low voltage spots have become very popular and no theatre that I visited was without them, These are pageant type lanterns without lenses but with silvered 24-Volt bulb and parabolic reflector. Since a 500 Watt lantern with built-in transformer is much smaller than a conventional 1,000 Watt soft-edged spot, yet gives a greater light intensity, the future of these lanterns in the British theatre, particularly in cramped boom positions, seems assured. There arc obvious possibilities for low voltage profile spots, but the examples so far available are rather long in the lens tube for our application.

All front of house lighting is accessible and is carried on concealed ceiling bridges. There may be as many as five bridges as at the Hamburg Opera where there are 60 FOH spots of 2kW and 5kW sizes, and in vertical side towers, frequently running from floor to ceiling, built into the wall beside the orchestra rail.

Artists are often followed from the proscenium and auditorium bridges, but the following is done discretely with low powered soft-edged spots.

Upstage lighting is sometimes. carried on bridges but there is an increasing tendency to save hanging space by installing remote-controlled spots on the batten bars. The focus, pan, tilt and colour of these lanterns can be accurately preset from dials on the switchboard without looking at the spot or indeed switching it on.

All new installations of cyclorama lighting use fluorescent tubes with flickerless transistor dimming.

Upstage lighting is normally from portable towers about 16 feet high which can be wheeled quickly into position. At Gelsenkirchen, however, I was interested to find portable hydraulic platforms which could be raised rapidly to any desired height.

Continental lighting control diverged from British practice in the early 1930s when they abandoned the resistance dimmer in favour of the auto-transformer. The main reason for this was the demand in a repertory theatre for load independence on all circuits coupled with lower power losses when running circuits on check. Tracker-wire control was adopted for these dimmers, since it was easier to arrange for mechanical presetting on this than on the simpler lever system which was the feature of the British Grandmaster control. Transformers and tracker-wires were standard until about 1955 and since then all major Installations have been all-electric systems offering multi-presetting with thyratron valves or magnetic amplifier dimmers.

But this is the age of the transistor and every lighting technician with whom I spoke was watching the Silicon Controlled Rectifier developments in London and Frankfurt with great interest. Meanwhile the Magnetic Amplifier is firmly established in practically every major European opera house.

While the engineering is superb, I personally feel slightly disappointed that the control desk of the standard German version (with 40 installations from the Bolshoi to the new Sydney Opera House) should reflect a miniaturisation of the old manual boards rather than the attempts to re-think in terms of the possibilities of modern solid-state electrical systems which has characterised recent Swedish, Belgian and English work.

Most new theatres have sited their control rooms in auditorium positions with excellent views of the stage, and transistorised radio provides communication between all members of the lighting staff.

The installations are operated, not by the casual labour system of our English theatres, but by trained theatre technicians who, provided they pass the necessary examinations, can be offered a permanent, progressive and pensionable career.

And what of the lighting achieved with all this splendid equipment? It is much bolder, less discreet, than ours: it slashes boldly across the stage in decisive directional strokes. I frequently felt an impulse to dash at the lanterns with diffusers or sheets of frost and to tone down the excesses of crude colour including the harsh whites. But was my impulse right?

Our English lighting has developed tremendously during the past decade, but are we going in the right direction? In our drift towards apricot smoothness, do we tend to forget the boldness that characterises true theatre?

New Glyndebourne lighting (1964) – from *The Stage*

The tour of large and small opera houses in Germany, Austra and Belgium was the first step in planning a new lighting control system for Glyndebourne. The system was used throughout the 1964 summer festival season.

There were two main influences in the planning of the system. One was a  statement by Peter Hall who, in

Glyndebourne lighting desk in 1964

his introductory address to the 1961 ABTT Theatre Conference, said: "Recently I had to produce the actors to suit the switchboard and it was necessary to instruct an actor not to move or say his line until he had seen number ten on the spot bar go out. Any alteration in his timing would have resulted in the next four lighting cues going wrong."

The other was the constant reiteration by Fred Bentham to the effect that lighting control would not advance very far until lighting men threw

Glyndebourne stalls rehearsal control in 1964

their microphones away and worked out the lighting directly on the levers of the control desk. The number 29 at a half ... up two points ... down half a point routine is inevitable in the West End where the lighting specialist leaves after the opening night, but it seems cumbersome in a repertory theatre with a resident lighting director.

Thus the two priorities in the design of the system became:

1. speed flexibility and
2. the possibility of operation by the lighting designer.

Other important requirements were

a. adequate presetting facilities,
b. clear indication on the desk of present and future states of the lighting,
c. ease of plotting and (d) ease of going back at rehearsal.

Lack of speed flexibility in most of the existing systems arises from the use of mechanically driven dimmer banks which, although allowing control of the overall speed of the whole cue, do not permit overlapping of cues or speed differentials within cues. Mechanical banks have been inevitable until recently because reliable solid-state dimmers have only been developed in the past few transistorised years.

The new instillation was based on 120 Thyristor dimmers, each of which will control any load up to 5kW: flexibility is ensured by a patch panel and 375 stage outlets. Strand Electric has led Europe in the development of these dimmers, although they have been used in television at home and abroad, Glyndebourne was the first European theatre to use thyristors and they have more than fulfilled the confidence placed in them.

The control desk in the production box at the rear of the circle has an uninterrupted view of the stage. The master desk forms a continuation of the producers desk enabling producer and lighting director to discuss lighting changes as they happen. This is possible because the operation is so simple: the lighting director merely moves the appropriate master levers in the way and at the speed that he wants the ·change to take place.

The preset wing allows four complete states of the lighting to be programmed: the 480 miniature levers have internally illuminated scales which glow when they are alive to give a visual picture of the present and future states of each circuit.

For rehearsal purposes two portable units can be set up quickly in the stalls. One is a duplicate master panel allowing any cue which has been preset in the control box to be performed from the producer's position in the stalls. The other unit is similar in appearance but in function to a single preset. Pressure on the scale of an individual lever operates a switch which transfers control of that particular circuit to the appropriate stalls lever, the scale lighting up to indicate that the stalls lever is now alive. An all-change push transfers all circuits to the stalls and a cancel push makes any circuits which have been taken over by the stalls revert to the main control.

An integrated intercom system allows the two desks to communicate with each other, with the prompt corner, and with all the electricians by means of inductive loop radio. The equipment is operated in the following way: when lighting a production, the lighting director, sitting in the stalls with producer and designer, builds up each lighting state using the levers of the stalls wing. As each state is established it is read-off to the control box where it is plotted and set-up on the main preset wing. The actual cue can then be tried on the stalls masters and its speed determined.

At rehearsals the lighting director plays the cues on the stalls masters and can try instant adjustments of any circuits by taking over on the stalls preset.

At performances the lighting director operates from the production control box. In other words, wherever the producer goes the lighting man and his levers are beside him.

The system appears to work. Apart from the tremendous time saving – in rehearsal the lighting can get back quicker than the orchestra can turn back their music – and the ease with which ideas can be tried and discarded, it is wonderful to be able to plot without worrying whether the board will be able to cope.

Down with the proscenium arch – A Dublin Case History (1974)

Tuesday, 5th November. Olympia Theatre, Dublin. Plotting lighting of *West Side Story* when there is a rumbling noise from top of OP Prosc Arch. Some plaster and rubble falls into prompt corner (it's a bastard prompt in the Olympia). The mess is swept up and sundry gents appear throughout the subsequent cues to peer up into the flys. Plot call lights and proceed to the pub next door.

Midway through lunchtime, theatre is deserted except for a couple of ASMs on stage setting up props for dress rehearsal and MD (Ed. Coleman) writing guitar part in stalls bar. A rumbling noise. Main RSJ supporting the proscenium arch (opening, I think about 34') slips and tears down box fronts. Proscenium brickwork and plaster follows and this brings down ceiling plasterwork. Roof rafters and timber walkway follows; as if hinged on the gallery end of the auditorium, it slams down across dress circle front. Orchestra pit and stalls area full of enormous piles of brick and plaster rubble. Orchestral instruments (piano, celeste, timps, percussion and sundry small instruments) become tangled wrecks and indicate the scale of human damage that would have been incurred in performance or even rehearsal.

Building evacuated, police guard, etc, etc, and all main services rapidly disconnected in view of fire risk. Immediate decision to proceed with opening that same night on schedule in suburban cinema which, a couple of weeks previously, had a run of *Joseph's Technicolour Waistcoat* on a scaffolding stage. New band parts flown from London, musical instruments borrowed. Costumes salvaged and a few props. Mini 24, FOH stage lighting towers, stands and a couple of CSI limes installed.

Proscenium and roof collapse at Olympia Theatre, Dublin

Opening terrific atmosphere because cast neurotically tuned and audience wanting it to work (big publicity cleared front pages of evening papers plus radio and TV had set scene).

How did it happen? Building said to have been inspected by surveyors three weeks previously and given safety clearance for licensing purposes. Inspection subsequent to fall suggested that keystones on which RSJ had been resting were of an inferior stone which had been deteriorating for some 80 years, but this was masked by plaster work. There had been some recent trouble with plaster work on the audience side of the proscenium and indeed a small scaffold was in position on the OP side to remedy this.

Why did it happen when it did? FR (who is not a surveyor nor an architect and is untrained and unqualified in all respects and therefore should not theorise on any subject) of course has a theory. On both proscenium pillars, *West Side* had rigged temporary scaffolding to support massive loud speakers of the type associated with pop. The sound at Monday night's dress rehearsal was conspicuous by its quantity (as we are well known to possess cloth ears, we will not comment on its quality). If the keystones were gradually disintegrating over the decades, were the frequencies of these speakers enough to hasten doom?

I understand that the roof has now been shored up with scaffolding to prevent further collapse, the two halves of the roof remained standing by a process of mutual support. The press carried all sorts of statements arising out of optimism. "Open for Pantomime". "About £15-20,000 damage". This is balls. To put the Olympia right will require massive restoration and if Messers Guinness will fund this, I will undertake to double my annual consumption of their stout product (I could not for a chain of restored opera houses bring myself to sup their marketing man's lager).

The total fabric of the super old theatre did not look too healthy: those of us who have worked there, while loving the building, can hardly be surprised that it all fell down. So what now? I hope that this does not spark off any licensing hysteria. On the other hand, I want someone to assure me that it couldn't happen here. That behind the splendidly maintained plaster work of my favourite theatres there lurks not a lump of crumbling sandstone.

For the record, this is my third escape (disregarding the frequent rain of spanners from tallescopes). Number 1 was in the Palace Devizes where three feet of steel scaffolding fell from the pocket of a cut-cloth and just grazed the tip of my nose. Number 2 was in Glyndebourne where a massive *Rosenkavalier* chandelier fell on to the spot where I normally stood throughout the scene change (I had moved only because a 223 had developed a droopy fork, and subsequently I have always had a soft spot for Patt 223s and their droopy forks).

India (1986)

India is a vast and complex country: it would be foolhardy to try to draw any meaningful conclusions about theatres, their lighting and sound, from a three-week tour of the southern states. Indeed priority for the eyes and ears of a first time visitor is inevitably the vibrant images of Indian life rather than any mere theatre which might reflect that life. However, since my journey was a specifically theatre one undertaken on behalf of the British Council to share my experience of design and technology with theatres and university drama departments, I suspect that I saw as wide a range of stages as is feasible in the time available.

Indian theatre tradition is more deeply rooted and continuous than that of the west. The prominence of the Greeks in our received notion of stage history is a result of the prominence of playwriting in their literature, and the durability of their theatre architecture. Indian theatre has not many monuments of the period prior to the arrival of the British with their proscenium arch. The creation of performance space was part of the total performance ritual and many of the traditional ritual dramas of the state of Kerala have recently been researched and documented by the

Indian Welcome

School of Drama at the University of Calicut. The importance of their extensive videos is not just the performances where the actors become the characters with a truth often sought after but never achieved in the west. (Anyone who doubts this statement should consider which western actor

Museum Theatre Madras

can become so godlike as to eat a live chicken.) To those interested in the visual aspects of theatre, the particular excitement of this video archive is the detailed accounts of the preparations to make and decorate the performance space, props and costumes. And then to destroy everything in a 'get-out' that is instant and total.

Today's Indian theatre is re-examining its roots and prominent among a generation of dramatists drawing inspiration from this deep cultural heritage is Sankara Pillai, director of the Kerala traditional drama research project. His CULT (Calicut University Little Theatre) plays the new drama (as well as international classics such as Waiting for Godot) in the Malayalam language, using some formal theatres but, I suspect, happiest in the delightful open air playing spaces with which India abounds. A banyan tree, a rock outcrop, a few stones, some bamboo, a fragment of soft brick wall are just some of the found objects which can make a cleared space into a theatre. A few simple focus spots lashed to a tree branch or hung from a bamboo tower produce effects that must call into the question the vast lighting rigs of the west.

But there has also been a lot of big theatre building, particularly during the last decade. How about their lighting?

Three weeks in the Southern Indian states revealed a few yards of S batten and some floods including the pattern 60 which augmented the Madras moon under which I lectured with slides of Gemini and Galaxy to an audience who could not let their aspirations extend beyond two presets and a pack of thyristor dimmers.

But restraining one's aspirations to realistic levels places no constraints whatsoever on creative imagination. Everywhere I went, I found Indian theatre people eager to embrace the ideas of the new technologies and use them in the service of performance. Conversations frequently revealed a perception of the creative possibilities of the new equipment that I often find missing in many of us, myself included, who have become so accustomed in our relatively affluent societies to the march of science that we use it as an alternative to creative thinking.

The spotlights that I saw were mostly simple PC lensed focus spots. With careful centering of reflector and lamp, the light can be smoothed out even if the lens glass, coupled with dimmers whose maximum is less than full, ensure that open white is tinged with rather more than a suggestion of gold. (It took me back to my own early years at the

Playhouse in Tonbridge and the Clinton Hall in Seaford.) Fresnels tend to spray their light with a generous abandon appropriate to a studio rather than the selective need of a stage. Barndoors are as rare as a monsoon in Iceland.

There are some gated and shuttered lens assemblies available as an optical add-on to the lamphouses of simpler spotlights, but their light suffers from the compromise optical system utilising a simple spherical reflector to collect light from a basic ES lamp. Some new profiles use a less than ideally shaped halogen lamp and have shutters that bring tears to your fingers, but they can be coerced into giving a rather useful light – with the possibility of gobo texturing which so rightly excites anyone who has previously been denied aceess to the necessary optics.

I was surprised to find no simple liquid or resistance dimmers. The standard for Indian dimming is the autotransformer – either a collection of individual rotary Variacs or grouped as interlocking portable of six to ten ways. All the permanent installations that I saw, even in the largest theatres, were made by grouping up these portables in a U formation with 40 ways as a large installation. However, at 5kW per channel this represents a lot of copper to carry the loads between the stage and the control room at the back of the auditorium in a1500 seat theatre.

Most of the new theatres have their lighting control rooms placed in ideal positions and have very good ceiling lighting bridges and side wall lighting positions. Installing new equipment will be a relatively painless exercise, except for the budget and electricity supply. Rapid expansion of electric distribution has led to a supply which can be prone to unscheduled blackouts and erratic in maintaining its designated voltage. Consequently, stand-by generators and voltage stabilisers are integrated into normal life as standard practice.

But let no one think that the basic nature of any of the equipment limits the possibilities of first rate lighting design. Imagination will always continue to draw the maximum effect from the most primitive resources. The performances of CULT (Calicut University Little Theatre), whether in a garden in Madras or a room in Trichur, used lighting in a way that was totally integrated with the acting, movement and music. It was almost impossible to believe that the sources were primitive spots lashed to a tree branch or peeping through a window, cross-fading so smoothly that surely an octopus must be handling the assortment of rotary Variacs laid out on a table. If such artistry is possible under such conditions, what could these lighting designers create with some newer technology? Let us not forget that by the time the Greeks were inventing theatre, the Indians had been performing for centuries.

India has a rapidly developing electronics industry and I think it reasonable to anticipate that the thyristor and memory revolutions which took place consecutively over the decades of the 60s and 70s in the west, will be compressed to happen simultaneously in the closing yeas of the 80s in India. My dearest wish for my new friends in Indian stage lighting is that import restrictions will be relaxed sufficiently for the experience of the west to be made available. It is fatally easy to write a plausible yet inadequate programme for a microprocessor, or to devise an unstable thyristor dimmer circuit that is frightened by projector lamp filaments.

And as for spotlights – well, a cautionary tale … After several days of demonstrating the facts of light with basic focus spots, my eye espied a pattern 23: that darling with whom I have been consumating lighting designs since 1954 and with whom I still enjoy many a geriatric flirtation. I pounced on the sleek form, offered some electricity and started to tweak her shutters and slide her lens. Alas, her light did not gladden my eye, her beam would neither harden nor soften properly and her shutters acted as dimmers rather than shapers. Moral: you can copy a casting superficially, but the lens and reflector need to be real rather than just look real.

Singapore (1990)

There is no talk of recession in Singapore. The growth rate of the economy is more than adequate to sustain wage increases ahead of inflation. The standard of living has a target of parity with Switzerland and there is every indication that this bullseye will be hit very soon.

Singapore does not fit into any of the ideologies of conventional political thinking. Massive social engineering runs in tandem with a market economy which is totally profit orientated, and particularly unique is the way in which state-run enterprises generate operating surpluses.

In its first 25 years as an independent republic, Singapore has exploited its geographical assets with exceptional skill and the proceeds have been reinvested in a model infrastructure. This is an urban environment which, although densely populated, fulfils many a dreamer's vision of a garden city. I do not know whether it is the cleanest place on earth, but I have

Victoria Theatre, Singapore

certainly never visited anywhere cleaner.

How fares Singapore theatre? The scene is lively and poised for expansion. When a successful planned economy turns its attention to improving the recreational aspects of the quality of life, the drawing boards start to hum with new projects and there are signs that Singapore will become one of the major international centres of theatre building activity in the 90s.

The first National Theatre of 1963, a large open air auditorium with covered stage, has already fallen to road widening and a cinema has been adapted to provide an interim house for the larger shows. The 1,800 seat auditorium of this Kallang Theatre is somewhat bleak, but the stage would satisfy the aspirations of any major British touring company. A prominent site has been allocated and planning is underway for a new Arts Centre complex which is likely to include three theatres offering alternative capacities and formats. Rumour has it that the Drama Centre, a 300 seat proscenium house, will also go in a redevelopment scheme, but the future of the historic Victoria Theatre is assured since it is at the centre of the preserved colonial heart of the city.

A 50s' refurbishment reduced the auditorium to a functional hall with cinematic sightlines and some of the that period's obligatory exposed concrete although most surfaces have been clad in timber panelling. It is to be hoped that eventually there will be a restoration to the spirit of its 1862 opening: perhaps not in decoration but certainly in format.

Other new venues on the drawing board include a University Theatre and there will be extensive facilities in the performing arts school to be included in a proposed new installation with the rather alarming title of Academy for Creativity Training. Meanwhile La Salle College is introducing a three year course leading to a professional diploma in drama.

In advance of building its new theatre, the National University of Singapore has launched an umbrella organisation to provide facilities for homeless theatre companies. Sponsorship has been raised for the salaries of coordinating staff, and the university will absorb costs of office space, clerical staff, telephones and other office equipment. Free rehearsal and performance space will be provided in existing campus facilities, the university will let companies keep all-ticket revenue and some production subsidies will be available.

A recent important addition to the Singapore scene is The Substation, an arts centre converted from a disused electricity transformer house, with facilities including a flexible studio theatre and an outdoor performance space called The Garden.

Act 3, the children's theatre company, has its own theatre where it was interesting for an old pantomimer like me to see Aladdin through South-East Asian eyes. And when the legendary Raffles Hotel reopens at Christmas, a new theatre will complement the gin slings and the legendary billiard table under which Singapore's last tiger is alleged to have met its bullet.

Most Singapore professional actors also have non-theatre second jobs: the drama companies have not yet developed to the point where they can offer their members a full-time living. Consequently there is a particularly high level of enthusiastic dedication; and it is heartening to find the leading companies determined to take artistic risks despite the considerable temptation that there must be to play safe.

Particularly prominent is Theatreworks with an impressive record of adventurous work since their launch in 1985. Their programming has not only included major international classic and contemporary plays but they have encouraged new writing by local authors. Indeed the current Theatreworks season included an eight play retrospective of Singapore drama written during the last 30 years.

The season also included a big new musical, *Fried Rice Paradise*, and will conclude with *The Trojan Women* played in a local quarry. The hottest ticket for *Trojan Women* is a dawn performance with buses collecting the audience at 5.45am. The sun will rise during a performance which will be followed by breakfast in the quarry.

Theatreworks policy is to perform in whatever local theatre is most appropriate for a particular production. However the company has now been provided with a home base in the impressively restored colonial Fort Canning. Administrative, storage and rehearsal spaces are adjacent to a 100 seat studio theatre – an open space with a lighting grid – appropriately named the Blackbox.

Although Singapore has four official languages – Malay, Mandarin, English and Tamil – English is the one that everybody understands. So it is the language of all road signs and most theatre performances.

British language and culture is fostered by a local British Council office which is particularly active in helping to catalyse the current theatre expansion.

My own presence in Singapore was to conduct a lighting design workshop with 15 enthusiasts drawn from the various theatres and production companies. Fourteen days of exploring stage lighting through intensive discussion and discovery projects using three different theatre spaces – just one of a series of British Council sponsored workshops running throughout 1991 and covering most aspects of writing, acting and production. Yes, today's Singapore has quite a theatrical tingle. And, of course, it is not free from controversy. There is considerable agonising among the local theatre community about the risk that the planned new big theatres may institutionalise the experimental spirit of the developing companies that are currently sufficiently small and flexible to be able to live dangerously and take artistic risks. They certainly want new theatre buildings but, having every true theatreperson's fear of monuments, they hope for flexible spaces on a human scale.

However, I did detect in the arts authorities a definite wish and intent to house Singapore theatre in a way which will allow it to develop its own indigenous form whatever that may turn out to be.

Kalami (2001 to 2008)

All holidays are memorable – not necessarily always happily, although all ours certainly were – with the most memorable being the dozen plus that we spent in Kalami. The balconies of the apartments built into the Corfu hillside overlook the village with its two swimming pools, two shops and four tavernas, one of which is in

Kalami

the house where Gerald Durrell wrote *My Family and Other Animals*. The one road into the village is neither a through road nor wide enough for buses. A pair of elevators provide access from the apartments to the village.

Return to Singapore (1992)

A couple of years ago, I reported the Singapore theatre scene as lively and poised for expansion. Well, the design computers are now multi-megabyting so that piling can start for the new Singapore Arts Centre, scheduled for a 1999 opening to usher in the millennium with a cultural flourish. This is not your average arts centre, not even just a big one, this is *The Big One*. A whole street of performance venues: concert hall, opera house and three theatres of assorted size and format. And in a row on a prime waterfront site at Marina Bay.

Singapore Sling

Although having a distinguished track record in public architecture, James Stirling and Michael Wilford Associates (in tandem with the local firm of DP Architects) do not immediately spring to mind as experienced theatre builders. But the design team includes Theatre Projects and Artec Consultants. With the likes of Iain Mackintosh and Russell Johnson on board, we can be reassured that any creative tensions will be positive, and with a bit of luck (it would be dangerous to deny that any theatrical endeavour needs luck) we can look towards performance friendly spaces parcelled within a dramatic statement about the nature of civic monuments in a new century. It is interesting to note that the commercial component of the development will include an Arts Village to house arts-related trades.

But Singapore has no intention of sitting back to await the opening of its megalithic temple to the performing arts.

The Victoria Theatre lighting has been refurbished with Galaxy Nova controlling an extensive rig featuring most of the Strand catalogue plus a batch of Clay Pakys and Super Troupers. Let's hope that, while Iain Mackintosh is commuting to the new Arts Centre site, the Victoria will seek his advice on restoring their auditorium to match the colonial heritage splendours of the area around the Padang – upon whose hallowed pavilion veranda your scribe, the most non-cricket of persons, partook of an excellent luncheon. The National University's new theatre is getting closer, and the Chinese High School has just completed a drama stage which has in their campus facilities that would upgrade many a city, including the one I live in.

The Substation and Black Box continue to thrive, with Theatreworks encouraging new writing through a workshopping programme which leads to a high proportion of their season being devoted to indigenous Singaporean drama on contemporary themes. Western opera flourishes at the Kallang Theatre in the gaps between Andrew Lloyd Webber and Cameron Mackintosh.

But perhaps the most exciting current initiative is the Arts Housing Scheme, a subsidised programme to provide arts groups with a home where they can develop their activities. The National Arts Council secures heritage-type buildings and funds basic rehabilitation costs. These properties, often in shell form ready for specialised outfitting, are let to arts groups at affordable rent for performance, rehearsal and administrative space. A few years ago Singapore was poised on the brink of destroying its architectural heritage in the name of progress. But the bulldozing was stopped a few minutes after the eleventh hour and many historic shop-houses have been preserved for eating, exhibiting and acting.

Raffles Hotel has been magnificently restored or, perhaps more accurately, re-built to the original plans. The flavour has just a tiny tinge of theme park, but this is the commercial reality of restoring a low rise hotel on a high rise island. The inevitable is acceptable when done with such classy panache. I certainly got a big kick out of sipping my Singapore Sling in the billiard room while tapes of Noel Coward offered *Mad Dogs* and *Mrs Worthington*. This being the market-led 90s, the waiter enquired whether Sir would care to take the glass home, only another $15. The sight of a packaged take away glass presented on the same tray as the sling might have induced fatal apoplexy in Somerset Maugham and inspired a ditty from Noel Coward, but I have to say that it was proffered with impeccable style. (Not even the Raffles Museum sells cans of pre-mixed Singapore Sling but you can get them in the airport duty free).

The new Raffles includes the Jubilee Hall theatre, seating 392 in upholstered luxury. A pleasant venue for daily multimedia presentations on the history of Raffles set against the story of Singapore, followed by an evening programme of plays and recitals.

Pity that its late Victorian design has the flavour of America rather than Europe. It is certainly very nice as it is, but an auditorium in the English Colonial tradition would have been even cosier and (surely a spur to Singaporean economic ethics) would have held more audience in the same space.

The Singapore theatre scene remains one based on accelerating growth. But where is Singapore going to find all the acting, dancing, singing and technical people for its expanding arts and entertainment industry? A five-venue Arts Centre will require an army of highly trained imaginative people if the community is to benefit from its massive investment in technology.

My own three week presence in Singapore was part of an ongoing in-service training programme developed as a joint initiative between Theatreworks, the National Arts Council and the British Council. It was heartening to find how much the students on my course had developed their lighting design skills in the two years since my last visit. There is a lot of theatrical talent in Singapore but it needs to be nursed within a more structured educational framework. Plans for a performing arts academy foundered when the scale of the proposal escalated towards a level of grandeur in keeping with its rather alarming title of Academy for Creativity Training.

Expansion and upgrading of facilities in existing institutions, followed by selective overseas study may well produce the performers. But staffing (back and front) the 1999 street of venues will require more drastic action. It really seems to call for the setting-up of a School of Theatre Design, Technology and Administration. With new venues planned throughout the Pacific Rim, Singapore is well placed geographically and economically to build an income generating regional facility. If it did the job properly – and Singapore, like Hong Kong, usually does a job properly – such a school could reach international standing at the same time as Singapore's Millennium Arts Centre

Singapore's Esplanade – Theatres on the Bay (2003)

I can find no trace, nor do I have any memory, of writing about Singapore's magnificent theatre – probably because it opened at a time when I had tired of reviewing theatre buildings. A few months after its opening, when the inevitable pace of opening had quietened, I was invited to conduct workshops on three days when the stage was dark. Notes which I prepared for the participants summarise many aspects of theatre lighting and so they are to be found in Chapter Three.

Theatres on the bay, Singapore

2 COMMENTS

Shall I see it from the box office? (1981)

What happens when a lighting man gets his hands on a theatre's budget?
When I arrived in Bury in 1959, I looked over the lighting equipment. It
was rather tired, both optically and mechanically. Cable tails were frayed
and earthing notional. There seemed to be only two possible alternatives:
to replace the lot or to kit out cast and crew in Wellington boots! I looked
in the cheque book: it might have stood replacement at 1950 prices. I
looked in the programme: *Merry Widow*. In wellies? Perhaps. But not in
Bury St Edmunds.

So I consulted a congenial gentleman named, rather oddly but aptly, A.
Lights, Esq. Ancient, for that was his Christian name, looked briefly up
at the hanging rig and instantly quoted a flat price per lantern for going
through the lot, replacing anything that was substandard: tails, holders,
reflectors, lenses, etc. I did an equally hasty calculation (using the seat
of my pants rather than more conventional accountancy) and accepted
by uttering that well known theatrical business expression – done! A pair
of ancient lightermen, equipped with a trolley loaded with bins of every
conceivable Strand spare and screw, whipped through the lot in a day.

You may wonder why we did not do the job ourselves ('in house' as
the jargon has it). Well, reference to 'Sod's Encyclopaedia of Lighting
Law' will confirm that diagnosis cannot precede dismantling. We did
not wish to invest in a comprehensive stock of spares, and our friendly
local stockist was hardly just around the corner. So I applied one of
the basic principles of budgeting and scheduling that is part of any
lighting designer's knowledge of management: reduce the unknowns by
subcontracting the risk and the hassle.

With safety restored, I hoped that I could forget all about the lighting.
The last thing that I wanted to do with my theatre's slender cash resources
was to spend on peripherals like marginally improved illuminations!
Survival for 350 seat theatres in isolated market towns of 27,000 souls
can only be based on buy shows cheap, sell them dear, bang the drum and
squeeze the overheads. The best available shows, well publicised, are the

only hope of attracting an audience. New lighting equipment? Would I see it from the box office?

However, there were disturbing bulletins from the control room. Elsie was reported to be sick. Indeed, terminally ill. So I went up to the gallery and gave her a good kick. My roots are in an earlier technology and so are Elsie's, so she perked up considerably and went about her daily cues in a more or less orderly fashion.

To those unversed in the christening procedures for older Strand boards, I should perhaps explain that Elsie was an LC ('Elsie', 'LC' ... get it?). For years I assumed that the letters L and C stood for inductance and capacitance. It was only years later, in the ante room of Strand's research and development department (the saloon bar of the Lamb & Flag) that I discovered that LC had been named after her midwife – an abbreviation for Legett's Choke.

Elsie's stage debut was the opening of Chichester Festival Theatre where she was immediately embraced by those of us who found the popular organ desks to be but Grandmasters robbed of their traditional multi-operator flexibility. In fact LC (2-preset, 3-group) was the grandmother of all today's controls whether they be multi-preset or infinite-preset (and I am definitely not referring to choke dimmer's unfortunate habit of remembering a fading vision of the previous cue!).

But logic was niggling away in my mind. Elsewhere in the theatre's operation, I was fighting a recession with a policy of you have to spend to make. I knew that capital expenditure on a new control would effect savings in running costs, but I think it was probably the fact that I was a lighting designer turned theatre administrator that was stopping me from spending money on lighting.

As usually happens, the decision was made for me. One opening night, I was gently enjoying the Victorian charms of *Lady Audley's Secret* complete with an admirable simulation of gaslight. The interval revealed that the random rippling of the light was not part of the lighting design, but was Elsie's involuntary contribution to the plot. Elsie received another therapeutic kick and normal working was resumed. But we had to accept that her end was nigh. We tried a Variac transplant but the donor turned out to be of a different mark. I appeared, with Elsie's support, in a one man show entitled *Lighting the Stage – all seats 50p, all receipts towards a new lighting control*. The publicity primed the local authority pump to the extent of a £10,000 interest free loan. Housing the Arts coughed up another £1,000 and box-office surpluses provided the balance.

We went to tender and were relieved when Duet 2, which seemed to offer the right facilities, turned out not only to be the cheapest quote, but within our budget – provided that we used some of our summer slack for do-it-ourselves installation.

The basic package was a Duet with VDU and pin patch. The choice of pin patch rather than twin preset was not made for back-up reasons. We hoped and believed that no multinational was going to market a packaged control that was susceptible to failure. Our faith was justified: 18 months continuous service so far without a single problem since installation. No, our choice of pin patch was because of a belief that this is the best facility for instant lighting of the one nighters who frequently fail to provide a running order, let alone a lighting plot.

Furthermore on some of these shows there is better contact if the lighting operator is on the side of the stage rather than in a remote control room. Also, any stage inevitably has some very simple evenings when an operator is unnecessary: apart from economics, it is not exactly humane to send anyone into a lighting box for two hours or more just to check the houselights and raise a preset when the pianist enters. So the pin patch masters were duplicated in the prompt corner.

The other act of economic humanity was to install a rigger's control. This just has to be regarded as essential in any small theatre. Especially in one like Bury where the total technical staff (stage, flys, electrics, props, maintenance) is two people. (And in March 1981 we opened for 28 days, giving 31 performances of 16 different attractions). It is difficult to function effectively if half the staff is continually climbing the gallery stairs to flash a channel for focusing!

These two extras – duplicate remote pin patch masters, and a rigger's control – turned out to be incredibly cost effective. And the Duet performed that standard feat of all memory boards: reduced plotting time and therefore overtime. As well as that all important reduction of hassle.

So, Bury reinforced my conviction that in lighting, like most things, you have to spend to make. Or if you prefer to put it more profoundly – capital investment produces economies in running costs.

Just before I left Bury, I started to put into operation a plan to save running costs by concentrating on stocking only a small range of cheaper long life lamps. Calculations suggested that lamp savings would justify part exchanges of new equipment (using T11or T19) for old (using T/4, T/15 or T/16) within the same financial year. First indications seem to confirm that this course of action is correct.

Very few of the great developments in lighting came about for purely artistic reasons. Staff reductions and contributions from electricity supply boards on the changeover from DC to AC provided the first real stimulus for remote control development. And it was the commercial theatre that first adopted the lighting designer: essentially as a money saving device, to be later adopted by the subsidised theatre for artistic reasons.

So the moral is … if lighting designers (like me) want to get new equipment from administrators (like me) they should go easy on the quality but stress the width: don't bother to try to explain the visual improvements that will increase the box-office (they will), but concentrate on the much easier proof that the sun will shine on the overheads.

A plea for more optimum and less maximum (1989)

What hope is there for a lighting designer who believes that lighting is not really all that important? Or certainly not as important as we would all like to think it is?

I have to confess to a nagging worry that many of us theatre people get so blinkered about our own speciality that we lose sight of how it fits into the whole.

This is not new thinking on my part: the proportions of production time and money devoted to lighting have been causing me concern for more than 30 years. Indeed, as a young stage manager in the 50s, I got involved in lighting, not so much because of a passion to create, but a desire to try and get the action moving so that we could all go to the bed via the pub.

I am just as concerned today because I suspect that theatre currently stands poised on the brink of being a victim of the dinosaur syndrome. The danger is international. Any element of risk is now impossible on Broadway and inadvisable in the West End. But costs are not only a problem for theatres operating within a market-based economy: the generous subsidy levels of most central European countries are under increasing pressure.

The theatre world claims that its major growth area has been in quality. Few would deny the exciting surge of the 60s and early 70s. But the subsequent decade has been rather more notable for its expansion in the areas of technology and bureaucracy. Growth follows a natural progression from minimum to maximum and somewhere in between is an optimum where there is a flattening of the curve of improvement plotted against expenditure of time and money. The search for an optimum approach has never been attractive to people in creative fields like arts, politics and marketing. Minimum and (particularly) maximum are much more exciting than optimum.

And I get a growing feeling that those of us who work in performance technology have become so fixated on going for the maximum that theatre may be on the way to becoming so bloated as to be unable to feed itself.

The size of lighting rigs and the knob count on control desks has climbed resolutely upwards, while the labour saving potential of each new hardware development has been absorbed by growth in the numbers used. The best of our lighting design is as good as it ever was (no, the best of it is not better, although the 'go for maximum' syndrome needs to assume that it is better) but how about the routine middle-of-the-road stuff? It is certainly brighter. But are eyes and teeth always getting the visibility at the core of any actor support system? Which brings us back to balance: the more one works with light, the more one discovers how audiences are protected from escalating brightness by the automatic irises in their eyes. But how about sound, now increasing in loudness to the point where musical intervals are becoming compressed to vanishing point? So far, the only people to have succeeded in developing irises in their ears seem to be sound operators.

But light and sound is just one element of an overall maximum tendency. The ratio of management to actors has increased exponentially and much of this is due to invasion by that prime industrial virus of our age … the one that believes marketing to be more important than product. But a more sinister cause may be the cost of public accountability. How much of the nation's theatre budget is devoted to funding the machinery of public audit and the procedures of democracy? And what is the cost – in salaries, telephones and photocopies – of the protests that theatres make about their inadequate funding? (Mostly counter-productive: the theatre industry, which exists by communicating the subtle nuances of laughter and tears, seems quite incapable of giving a simple explanation of its own economics.)

Public accountability now includes the necessity to be seen to be seeking sponsorship. But what is the cost of touting for such money? Euphemisms abound. Can we really expect our theatre to develop when its development directors are executives who have been specifically hired to raise funds. Occasionally, we are given an indication of the subsidy and sponsored percentages of unit seat cost: we are never told what percentage of that percentage is devoted to the costs of seeking, granting and auditing. Not so many years ago, theatres were under-managed. Are some now over-managed? I have a strong suspicion that many have passed upwards through the optimum.

Perhaps we lighting people should lead the way by demonstrations of restraint. The desire to maximise is understandable. I am no stranger to the compelling wish to ensure the success of my contribution to a production by hanging lights for every contingency then adding a belt to the braces. But I have discovered time and time again that elimination of equipment through extended agonising during the planning phase tends to result in lighting that is not just cheaper, but cleaner and crisper. And, while I acknowledge that most of the knobs on the jumbo lighting boards were not put there for working the performance, but for speeding up rehearsals, it has been my experience that it is not the board that matters, but its operator.

My generation is lucky: our development proceeded in tandem with the growth in sophistication of the technology. For us it was a process of gradual discovery with a continual need to make priority decisions. But people taking up a theatre lighting design career today are thrown into complex technology without adequate preparation.

We have to develop our lighting education ... and I say 'education' rather than 'training' because we are talking, not just about understanding the possibilities of technology, but about developing visual sensibility. Our theatre needs lighting people with eyes and sound people with ears. And I believe that everyone – performers, directors, designers, technicians, managers – needs to know much more about each other's contribution. Only then can we hope for a theatre which is greater than the sum of its parts: a situation more likely when each of these parts is based upon an optimum rather than maximum or minimum use of resources.

But to return to my starting point: the importance of lighting. The crunch is that lighting usually only seems important when it is not very good or takes up more than its fair share of the budget and schedule.

Strand at 75 (1989) Some major Strand developments in performance lighting

It seems no time at all since that golden evening in 1964 when Strand invited 749 distinguished theatre persons plus the young me to join them in an attempt on the Dorchester's champagne record. It was indeed a golden moment in lighting history. Strand was not only celebrating a pretty successful 50 years of lighting past, but it had just started to make the key product of lighting future: The thyristor dimmer (then called SCR – Silicon Controlled Rectifier) had arrived and Strand was in the lead.

Europe's first TV thyristors were installed at the BBC and their first theatre installation was about to go into Glyndebourne. (I was at the party because I had placed the order.) At that jubilee we were not just celebrating 50 years of Strand achievement, we were waving a grateful farewell to all the dimmer anguish associated with resistances, transformers, chokes, valves and, yes, even drainpipes. (I personally did my last dimmer maintenance with a watering can at the old Scala – in Goodge Street, not Milan – in 1959, although their liquid pots survived for a few years more.)

However, the 1964 Strand, while masterminding the thyristor revolution, were already looking ahead to the memory revolution that would offer instant recording and recall of an infinite number of presets. But before remembering that trauma, let us look at some of the key moments of the pre-thyristor era: a personal selection, let me hasten to add. I have neither taken a punter's poll, nor consulted Strand's 'department of anniversary marketing'. I have not even bounced my list off Fred Bentham, now distinguished archaeologist, but throughout Strand's formative years their senior engineer, organist, anarchist and marketing guru.

I feel reasonably certain that Fred will approve my choice of playability as the feature that has marked Strand's successes in desk design. The key breakthrough in pre-electronic lighting control was the Mansell Electromagnetic Clutch which allowed a shift of emphasis from the technologically feasible to the operationally desirable. Henceforward

Grandmasters would increasingly become Grandservants. Strand's flair (and for Strand read Bentham) was not just the use of electromagnetic clutches to remote the dimmers, but the realisation that the musician's keyboard was a control surface with an impeccable field test record over many centuries. The Compton Organ not only had playable keys but electrical circuitry for assembling and moving lights in groups. It even had a group memory. The Light Console was essentially a group board: bringing individual channels to intensity levels required virtuoso finger-work until polarised relays became available for presetting the clutch limits in the 1950s.

While the motor driven dimmer banks could not dim proportionally (shortest travellers finished first) the actual timing was sensitively controlled by a foot pedal.

Several desk functions were duplicated for optional foot control, a technique last used on the Lightset (a splendid finale for manual presetting) but not carried into the memory era. I still find my feet useful in my car and I can remember a time when they were indispensable on my board. A case perhaps for a little bit of 'to move forward, first look back'?

Proportional dimming had to wait for J. T. Wood's Electronic with its two presets feeding an elegantly simple, if somewhat delicate, circuit using a trio of ex-radar triode valves. (The history of stage lighting, its present and almost certainly its future, depends upon latching on to devices developed for some other purpose with more sales potential than the stage.) Life with Woody's electronic was never less than exciting, particularly the stickers – dimmer failure keeping them on at full until somebody got to the racks. But its dipless crossfade was the way forward that most of us (including most of Strand) knew where we wanted to go – although thyristors were around for quite a few years before we finally got there. Indeed by then memory had arrived.

Strand was first with memory and got the basic philosophy right, not only opting for digital but using a very playable rocker-per-channel desk. This might have compensated for their lack of adequate engineering resources. But alas, they also failed to listen to user playback requirements and so Thorn snatched the honours with the Q-file. Strand responded with an unfortunate decision to go analogue, resulting in crates of temperamental analogue/digital converter cards. When the dimmers failed, the lights came to full; this may have been fail safe in a studio but was disaster on a stage. The IDM desk, with its dimmer per channel, earned a big order book but its technology required the resources of a company on the scale of Rank. (Did they know about IDM when they bought Strand?)

Soon there was DDM, still in my view the jewel in Strand's control desk crown. But it was MMS that made memory standard. Having burnt their fingers on the analogue problems of dimmer levers, Strand stuck with keyboards (and I nominate Galaxy as king in this league) until the recent advent

Fred Bentham at the Stratford DDM

of Lightboard M. Keyboard access is not as fast as rockers or levers, but how else do you handle hundreds of channels. Will today's Strand achieve a breakthrough akin to Bentham's Strand.

So much for control (please note I am drawing a veil over Junior 8 – my nerves could never cope with its switching system). How about lanterns? I personally prefer the American term 'instruments' but I grew up with the Strand word. Incidentally, did Strand invent 'lantern' or did they inherit it from Digby? I expect I'll get a postcard from Bentham or Legge on this one. I certainly dislike the word 'luminaire' almost as much as I dislike the phrase 'state-of-the-art'. (Woe betide any salesperson approaching me with a state-of-the-art luminaire!)

Any manufacturer's success with lanterns is dependent upon the lamp industry. This considerably delayed the arrival of ellipsoidals in Europe, but a spherical mirrored profile, the Pattern 23, gave Strand their number one hit of all time. It is no longer made but is still in widespread use – with a

Pattern 23

lively second hand market developing because there is no replacement from Strand or anybody else. (To those who protest, I would just say length as in short). When it first appeared some 40 years ago, Strand tooled up for die cast production, showing a confidence and courage, both technical and commercial, unique in the history of stage lighting manufacture.

With the great 60s' surge in theatre building came the 264. The lamp manufacturers had produced a slender sausage, burning cap up, to fit within an ellipsoidal reflector. Strand had one of their major brainwaves and doubled the shutters to ease the hard/soft focus option. This level of inspiration failed to arrive with the great halogen lamp revolution. The 764 was a diecast Leko front stuck on to a 265 lamp house. I was involved and accept some blame. My defence is that it was a stop gap which went on for too long (throughout its short development it was known as the 'interim'). The Strand profiles that followed were somewhat uneven, with the Prelude 16/30 being the only one to offer me any particular pleasure. But then Cantata came along, putting Strand back to the top of the class.

No Strand reminiscence is complete without the Pageant, the first incandescent lantern capable of putting any real 'oomph' on to the stage - especially in its initial version with glass reflector. Most of us wept and screamed at the end of the 50s when Fred decreed that we did not need our beloved pageants any more and manufacture was shut down.

However, the beam light family has always been a bit of a Strand blind spot. (They initially adopted such a toffee-nose disbelief in the importance of the Par 64 that it took them until quite recently to make an acceptable parcan). Another blind spot for years was low-voltage, rejected with fervour after a pre-war flirtation. So when I tried to place an order in 1961 for 24 Volt Beamlights, I was firmly advised by 29 King Street that if I wanted to indulge in such anarchy I should take Glyndebourne's chequebook to Berlin. Which I did. But times change and Strand have reached in 1989, a position to fulfil that order. I now look to them to lead, in due course, with the electronic transformer when it becomes viable.

And let's give them credit: leading is what Strand have been doing recently. Particularly in remote operation of lanterns (by the way I dislike the generic term 'intelligent lights'; I think of them as 'obedient lights') Frenzied movement with a strong random element is now old hat in entertainment lighting, but PALS has disciplined the action, achieving acceptable repeat accuracy with a system that can be applied to any kind of lantern. And the big leap into the future is that Galaxy handles pan, tilt, focus and scroll at the same time as intensity. The lighting desk has become the true servant of the stage. Will some operators wish to use their feet?

A final suggestion about looking back to move forward. Who remembers the Patt 265? It was the first CSI follow spot (400 Watt). I remember it well because I used four of the first batch for *Man of la Mancha* in 1968. The 265 was not just unique for its source but was the earliest of the lens variable beam angle profiles. And the lenses were linked to form a coupled zoom. Say no more, Francis.

Pattern 265

In proposing an anniversary toast to Strand we must not forget the hook clamp. Ye who have never rigged with its predecessors can never be fully aware of the impact of such an elegantly simple design concept in the development of stage lighting.

But theatre is a people industry and so it is with Strand. I will not risk a roll call but if I had to choose one single person to epitomise what I have always looked for and usually found in the old firm, I would nominate Eddie Biddle, engineer and artist. P.S. I have made no mention of Tabs – but it speaks for itself from our bookshelves.

Low Voltage Beams Their past, present and future

In my 75th Birthday tribute to Strand in last month's *Lighting + Sound International*, I welcomed their decision to take Britain into low voltage beamlight manufacturing. However, the promotional information which has just appeared in the Strandbook suggests to me that there may be need for some clarification about the use of this type of instrument as a long throw light. To anyone unfamiliar with low voltage beamlights (marketed by Strand as Beamlites) seeking guidance as to why they should buy them, Strandbook offers the following advice:

The new beamights with their integral transformers mounted axially to the lamp, make neat compact units, producing a five degree beam spread of very high intensity to create dramatic lighting effects over very long throws. Low voltage beamlights are widely used in continental Europe for general lighting, and are now finding increasing favour with UK lighting designers.

Beamlights 24volt, 500W and 1kW

Now there is nothing actually false in this statement but its selectivity could possibly mislead newcomers to this type of equipment. The economy of words necessary in writing catalogue copy requires care in choice of priorities and it is questionable whether long throw performance is the prime selling point of these lights. This is particularly so if a 5 degree cone is the nearest that pricing constraints will allow us to approach a truly parallel beam.

A beamlight is distinguished from all types of lens spotlight in that the light beam from a parabolic reflector is parallel rather than conical. A perfect beamlight would have zero beam angle and would therefore light the same area irrespective of throw. This is what has long endeared it to central European theatres as a discreet followspot. The beam from a standard

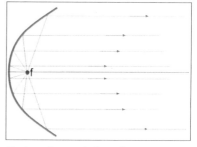

Optics of a parabolic reflector

sized reflector is just about the right diameter for head to waist, with just the right softening off towards the edges. It maintains this size as the throw changes – useful for all following, but particularly so for following from backstage positions when the throw can double during an actor's diagonal walk. Absence of lenses makes for an easily balanced unit, particularly if the transformer is mounted externally. Absence of lenses also helps to maintain light output, already high from a low voltage lamp.

Since a narrow beam is produced without the light losses inherent in a complex lens system, the beamlight becomes an attractive proposition for long throws. Therefore in huge theatres beamlights can find themselves used as substitutes for more conventional instruments for backlighting, side lighting and even frontal bash.

However, most of the excitement of beamlights comes from uses not specifically associated with long throws. My own love affair with low voltage beams dates from seeing them in action in German opera houses in the 1950s, and using them extensively myself at Glyndebourne throughout most of the 1960s.

The bright incisive concentrated beam made the beamlight a prominent feature of central European stage lighting, particularly in the east. It is an instrument which lends itself to a style based on high contrast directional lighting of the scenery from a relatively small number of sources, with the actors being separately covered by followspots from a series of appropriate angles, both front of house and on stage.

With sensitive operators, such a lighting style can be not only visually dramatic, but also appropriate in lighting management terms for a daily changing repertoire so large that extended gaps between performances can lead to singers being less than precise in taking up their stage positions.

Parallel beams do not easily lend themselves to the precisely defined lighting of acting areas. However, a series of beams can be butt joined to light an area with a sweep that can have more visual credibility than a single cone. Parallel beams, especially intense ones, tend to pick up any particles in the air and this helps to give the light a bite.

For most of the 1960s, I had 24V beam lights in my standard Glyndebourne rig: 500 Watts from side auditorium slots close to the stage and 250 Watts from the downstage booms. These were Reich & Vogel with a silvered lamp screwed through the centre of the parabolic reflector and no spill rings. Their transformer weight made them uncomfortable to rig, but once in position they were finely balanced for an easy twice-daily focus. And beam light focus is fast because, apart from pan and tilt, the only adjustment is a lamp centring knob to remove any central black hole. As a repertoire unit they could produce intense directional white swathes when working with the Germans, or the gentler, more colourful, although still highly directional light favoured by the Italians. Checked well down and colour corrected, they could even supply a bit of fill in the occasional production that just called for soft discretion.

Although an ideal beamlight would emit a pure parallel beam, design and manufacturing problems (particularly the production of a perfect parabolic reflector at a price that we would be prepared to afford) usually mean that the beam will emerge with some conical tendency. There will therefore be a certain amount of beam spread but as this is but a few degrees it only becomes significant on really long throws. Alas it is beam quality which tends to suffer and the extent is unlikely to be acceptable unless the desired effect is that of a splodge gobo.

In general I personally would rarely wish to use a beamlight (with the possible exception of a precision model purposely made for followspotting) on any throw much longer than that on which I would use a parcan. Indeed, parcans are a member of the beamlight family and when they first appeared, I immediately embraced them as downmarket beamlights. So with low voltage beamlights now available in Britain as an indigenous species rather than just an import, perhaps newcomers to this source might find it useful to think of them as upmarket parcans with a more biting, incisive. smoother and symmetrical oomph.

Into the nineties – avoiding a decadent decade (1990)

With each New Year the media parade the past and probe the future.

Filing systems and crystal balls are consulted in a search for significance. Phrases are coined. Labels abound. With the dawn of a new decade the pace of recall and forecast quickens. I await the turn-of-the-century with apprehension. But I play the looking back and forward game.

Will the basic trends of the 80s continue into the 90s? Will sound get louder, lights brighter, scenery heavier, bureaucracies larger and cuts deeper? Will our theatre be much the same, only more so? Or will it respond to the popular revolution now sweeping eastern Europe?

A flood of new writing can certainly be expected from the new democracies. But how will these new plays be staged? Eastern European productions since the war have been characterised by high visual imagination rather than advanced technology. But I'll bet the average Warsaw Pact theatre technician is hoping that western aid will include crates of goodies covered in hi-tech knobs and whistles.

In the final *Stage* of the 80s, Flyman offered us a 90s fantasy based, like all good farces, on underlying truths. His predictions may be impossibly Gothic in detail but they are frighteningly believable in spirit. The word 'decade' is alarmingly close to 'decadent'. What can we backstagers do as our contribution to avoiding a decadent theatre decade?

Perhaps we have to be less single minded about the importance of our own particular specialist contributions. Be prepared to concede that money for extra lights or microphones might be better spent on more rehearsals or bassoons. I know that in suggesting this I shall be accused of lowering standards. I can remember the full wrath of the 60s descending upon my head when I advocated fewer lights and more imagination. But we technicians just have to overcome our well justified cynicism and become more involved in the whole theatre process.

A wit described a production meeting at one of our underfunded institutions as everyone arriving with a shovel to dig their individual entrenched positions around the table. This is not to say that technicians should surrender their budgets to the marketing department without discussion. We must fight for a more democratic theatre with openly debated budgeting and scheduling. But to get it we perhaps need to put our own house a little more in order. Some areas in need of a fresh outlook include:

- Sound is getting better but has it improved in proportion to the money thrown at it? Why does it rarely seem to be coming from the actors' mouths? Why is it so loud?

- Light desks grow more and more knobs. We ask for them but does anybody use them? The latest spots each cost as much as the entire rig for a drama studio but do everything without a ladder. Will we use them as an efficiency tool to save time or add their manic swooping beams to the flashing, flickering and chasing that distracts audiences of dance and song?

- Scenery was at its most minimal when funding was liberal. Visual excitement has now been rediscovered but not illusion. Theatre has always used magic to produce so much from so little. Why have we let this become so little from so much? Weight and bulk escalate construction costs only a little, but handling and transport a lot. Our touring could learn from American bus and trucking.

We all talk a lot about training but there is little mention of education. Certainly there are specialised skills to be learned, but they are not much use unless taught in relation to theatre as a whole. Education, like theatre, is about discovery. Learning skills in a discovery environment was the basis of the old backstage apprenticeship system but today's theatre has so many formats that comprehensive on-the-job learning is no longer possible. So we need to develop an educational system which offers theatre workers regular opportunities to update skills, knowledge and discoveries throughout their careers. Our theatres need staff who are jacks of all trades and masters of one. And that applies as much to directors and administrators as to flymen and electrics. Most of our working difficulties are failures of communication due to lack of understanding of each other's skills, problems and contribution.

My hunch is that if our theatre in the 90s is going to rise above its current risk of boring its audience with tales of funding woe, we shall need to aim for a new democracy based on educated understanding and debate.

Malaysia (1995)

We backstagers are aware of sponsorship and we know it helps to keep us in work but, like marketing, it is just one of these many front office activities that we rarely get close to. However, for the first time in my life, I have experienced the benefits at first hand. ICI maintain a guest house in the posh part of Kuala Lumpur. Forget any thoughts of B & B or Basil Fawlty. This is high living in a colonial style villa dedicated to smoothing the travels of the chemical industry's movers and shakers. Their every need is anticipated by the legendary Mrs Marfuah, a lady who elevates the title of housekeeper to new heights of artistry.

The event which ICI was supporting was a ten day lighting design workshop, organised by the British Council in conjunction with the Malaysian Ministry for Culture, Arts and Tourism. Four different stages, including one recently completed Experimental Theatre, were used. Staff from all these venues participated in the full ten-day programme, as did members of the producing companies who use the facilities. It was therefore possible to relate practical projects and seminar discussions to the circumstances in which local theatre is produced.

It can be difficult to involve a group of 22 in practical project work, but this particular group integrated quickly and worked together for 65 hours with the cheerful friendly commitment that can be the delight of our theatre industry when its wheels are turning smoothly. Indeed, perhaps the major success of this workshop was providing an environment in which the resident technical lighting providers from the theatres and the itinerant lighting users from the production companies were able to reach a better mutual understanding.

In Malaysia, as in most countries with a rapidly expanding economy, theatre growth is seen as making an important contribution to enhancing the quality of life in tandem with increasing prosperity. The performing companies are enthusiastic and there is a lot of exciting production activity on well-equipped stages. There are lots of lighting ideas and lots of lights. This is top of the range equipment, but the absence of a developed methodology for using it to full benefit has triggered considerable frustration.

Sessions were in Kuala Lumpur, but I was able to fit in a Penang weekend where three theatres are under refurbishment, including a potentially exciting studio conversion from a retired rifle range at University Sains Malaysia. Not being an Englishman I must be a mad dog, for I braved George Town's scorching noonday sun to wander among the splendours of the local variants of traditional Chinese shop house architecture and the remains of the colonial glories of the East India Company. These include Drury Lane, the Eastern and Oriental Hotel, known as the E & O, where the unreconstructed bar, once propped up by Noel Coward and Somerset Maugham, exposes Singapore's restored Raffles as Disneyland.

At a political level, Britain's relations with Malaysia have recently been under a little strain. Working at a rather more grass-roots level, the visit brought home to me the way in which the arts can always continue to keep friendly communication alive during times that may be stressful in other areas.

Alumnus Alternatus – a University education without a degree

Famous for his rhododendrons, tall and gangling in his stiff wing collar, Sir William Wright Smith, Professor of Botany and Regius Keeper of the Royal Botanic Gardens, 73 and disinclined to retire, addressed we 1948 freshers in his rolling Scottish brogue.

Gentlemen (many of us were, in fact, ladies) Gentlemen, you are not here to gain qualifications for a job. You are here for the good of your minds and hopefully, in some small way, for the good of your souls.

I took him at his word and left four years later with a developed mind (certainly) and soul (hopefully) but no degree. An ordinary B.Sc. then required seven passes over three years. but in my four years of study I sat seventeen degree exams to get five passes, only three (Botany 1, Psychology 1 & 2) being gained without resit.

I may not have graduated with a degree but I had acquired an education. The facts of science may have eluded my understanding but its methodology would provide me with a logical approach to my subsequent career in theatre lighting design – a subject at the crossroads between art and science. While never missing a lecture or tutorial at the University, I was in the gods of the Lyceum every Saturday, the Usher Hall every Friday and either the Reid music school concerts or the King's Theatre every Thursday.

Without this width of education, I doubt whether I could have helped establish the new profession that enabled dramaturgy to absorb the surge of new technology in the second half of the 20th century. As theatre increasingly became a degree subject, it was inevitable that I was invited to teach in parallel with my stage work. I never quite became a proper academic – none of the fifteen books I contributed to my subject contain a single footnote! But as a course leader in a London Art School, a Dean in a Hong Kong Academy and a world traveller for the British Council, I managed to survive without a degree. But, thank you Edinburgh, I did have had an education.

While signing-off hundreds of degrees as an external examiner, I never forgot the magnitude of Sir Willie at my Botany One oral, waving a dried-up weed at me in desperation...

Man – can you no even recognise an umbelliferae!

At the door I was halted by:

Mr Reid!, Mr Reid, if by some extraordinary chance you were to gain a pass in this examination, would it be your intention to further pursue the study of Botany in this University?

No, Sir William.

Aye, well then, on the strict understanding that you never again enter these laboratories and never again visit my botanic gardens, even to admire the flora, I am prepared, in view of your extreme youth – for I perceive that you are barely eighteen years of age –

and with the acquiescence of the external examiner, reluctantly given, to grant you a pass in this examination.

I kept my promise and to this day I have never again crossed the threshold of the Royal Botanic Gardens.

A Scenic Art Tradition Revived (2007)

In the 18th and early 19th century, the role of scenic artist included the design and execution of the décor for both auditorium and stage. Indeed, in some cases this could even extend as far as the architect's role being limited to the provision of a shell to be fitted out by theatre painters such as the Bibbiena family who have left us a legacy crowned by the Margrafentheater in Bayreuth. So it is appropriate that the custom was revived during the restoration of the Theatre Royal at Bury St Edmunds to the spirit of its 1819 origins.

As proprietor of the Norwich circuit, it was natural that architect William Wilkins should entrust creative interpretation of his auditorium decorative concept to the renowned Norwich Theatre Royal artist, George Thorne, who would also equip the Bury stage with stock scenery. This tradition has been maintained by Meg and Kit Surrey who researched, designed and painted appropriate decorative treatments for architect Axel Burrough's restoration of the auditorium structure. Bury Royal is the only working theatre in the National Trust portfolio and so the Trust's experts were available to provide research advice, not just about paint but on classical sculpture for the restoration of the three muses, four seasons and three graces painted on the proscenium frieze. As themselves veterans of the powdered colour and glue size that would have been used in 1819, the Surrey's are "absolutely sure that if George Thorne had had acrylic paint available he would have leapt on it with the same joy with which we all took to using it the 1960s".

Whether painted in-situ, or on canvas in the studio and then appliquéd, as were the frieze and box fronts, the textural quality of the brushwork proclaims the building's theatricality and helps to link house to stage. This was especially so during the reopening production for which the Surrey's designed and painted perspective sets which slid, rose and fell in accord with the Georgian mode. *Although Black Eyed Susan* has a strong nautical basis, it may well be that some cloths and flats could join the theatre's act drop, in the spirit of the stock scenery tradition, for the Rediscovering the Repertoire seasons that are planned as a recurring feature of the programme.

Virtual Reality

Backstagers one and all, are you ready for a cyberspace world? Will you welcome Virtual Reality or do you feel threatened by it? Or perhaps you have not realised just what is in the minds of our directors, designers and marketeers?

As we backstagers devoted another festive season to bleeding through gauzes to reveal panto fairies wallowing in dry ice, what were the creative mob dreaming about?

Virtual reality goggles

My spies tell me that the tech rehearsals for a recent West End to Broadway transfer involved nine production desks. On five of these stood personal computers, one of which was chatting through a modem with its London mainframe. But we ain't seen nothin' yet.

When I was a lad, you had to have a gimmick. You still do, but now it is called an innovative creative response. So, unless you wish to remain stuck in a 20th century time warp, get measured for your sensor-laden bodysuit, electronic gloves and video goggles. Yes folks, it's time to respond positively to the pleading of the marketing pundits that you 'walk through the computer generated virtual reality that surrounds you, picking up and manipulating all the objects in this cyberspace world'.

Designers often despair at the inability of directors to visualise how the model will scale up to become a set (Is visual multiplication by 25 really so much more difficult than deconstructing the scripts of dead playwrights who are presumed not to know what they were writing about?).

But, despair no more. Director and designer can wear gloves and goggles to go walk about in the model. Admittedly their ability to walk on cardboard and move it around is likely to bring some grief for the production manager. But, let's face it, scenery became a bit of a lost cause when canvas flats and gate-leg rostra ceased to be fashionable.

Forget marking out the rehearsal room when you can computer generate a set which has virtual reality. Dress the actors, director and DSM in the gear and let them all get on with it in cyberspace. The DSM may wish to stay in her suit for the performances so that, suitably multiplexed, she can make virtually simultaneous visits to cue the flys and limes. (Between cues, flymen can use their gear to investigate any reports of reality, virtual or otherwise, in the front office.) But being serious for a brief moment. In a curious way, realism is usually more convincing on television than in live theatre where natural behaviour needs considerable heightening and strengthening to carry conviction. So, the ability of computer generated and manipulated images to get no closer to nature than being virtually real, is no block to their use as an element of theatric language.

Theatre is about interactions and virtual reality technology may possibly be a way forward. Certainly one deserving experiment.

Who will be the first to kit out an audience? After all, it is not such a big step from handing out cardboard specs for a 3-D movie. The ultimate in promenade performance. Or we could have some real audience participation: give the punters a real chance to screw up the show. Out would go 'It's behind yer!' to be replaced by 'It's virtually around yer!' If everyone had their own volume control, they could turn the sound down below its currently fashionable threshold of pain. Perhaps Alan Ayckbourn would write a play where each and every member of the audience could choose their own ending, or write their own if they didn't fancy the author's menu.

I thought I was fantasising until, in a break in *Cinderella* rehearsals, I saw the BBC Christmas edition of *Tomorrow's World*. They used Virtual Reality machines to turn Anneka Rice into a frog. This could be the greatest development in panto technology since the star trap. But it will never upstage a real pair of principal boy's legs.

Token Male (2009)

At the 1974 USITT annual conference in New York, Tharon Musser chaired a discussion on Careers for Women in Theatre Production. With the aid of an Arts Council bursary (happy days!) I had accepted an invitation to join a panel on Training Future Theatre Technicians and so, as the only British designer of any gender signed up for the conference, I was accorded honorary female status (no, they did not spell me as

Frances) for the afternoon and co-opted to offer some appraisal of of the current UK position.

Introduced by Tharon as 'Our Token Male', I reported that the vast majority of prompt corners were established female territory, and that women made a greater impact on set and costume design than their numbers might suggest, but lighting design remained a male preserve awaiting the equivalent of the successful assault that Peggy Clark and Jean Rosenthal had led on Broadway. The 1973 *Handbook of The Society of British Theatre Lighting Designers* listed 29 members of whom the only woman was Molly Friedel – and she was American as was Honorary Member Tharon Musser. I suggested, not wholly tongue in cheek, that this might perhaps result from feminine common sense in staying clear of a profession requiring maximum adrenalin without offering adequate financial reward.

Nevertheless the number of women in lighting crews, if still disappointingly small, was increasing and included many of our finest board and followspot operators. Attempting to burnish my own credentials in the matter, I pointed out that I had broken the male LX taboo at Glyndebourne by hiring an Australian girl in 1961.

There has been a lot of progress in the 35 years since that conference but equality remains elusive. So I am delighted that the ALD welcomes the initiative by Paule Constable and Sarah Rushton-Read to develop more support for women working in technical theatre. As a lighting designer, Paule understands the crucial importance of balance so I am confident that there is no imminent danger of us chaps being relegated to token status.

Can the art keep up with the science

Or will creativity vanish in a terminal frenzy of flash, flicker, rotate and chase?

My title may be rather wildly over dramatic. But we live in a world of hype where you need an ever increasingly polemic turn of phrase to get an ear … or an increasingly exaggerated light to catch an eye. However, even the wildest polemic statements are beginning to fail: extremes of language are becoming as blunted as extremes of light and sound. The window which electronic news gathering has given us on to the more extreme forms of mankind's survival has brutalised our senses

In polemic mood

... so it takes metaphorical sledgehammers to make any impression upon us. To anyone crying doom, doom and thrice doom, the reply is likely to be 'Have a nice day'. Lights get brighter and brighter and sound gets louder and louder in a search for levels that, in theory, cannot be ignored. But our perception becomes so dulled that we don't notice so much, and we see and hear less and less.

What is the future for our controlled manipulation of the light that we work, play or perform in? Can the art keep up with the science? Or will creativity vanish in that terminal frenzy of flash, flicker, chase and rotate, upon which I waxed poetical in the title of these musings. It may be a polemic suggestion ... but most polemics have at least a grain of truth.

I am not knocking the technological development: lighting technology is great stuff and I want more of it. My concern is what we do with it. What agitates my worry beads is that lighting seems to have got locked into hyping itself in order to get noticed. So desperate to get noticed – as if to survive – that it gets bigger, brighter, flashier, faster. An instrument that just gets blunter and blunter. Have we forgotten the dance of the seven veils? You don't drop them all at once. Reveal gently. Tantalise. The last one is often disappointing, but good timing will disguise that.

Has the technological means developed so fast that we might just be getting close to losing our creative use of all the lovely fruits of technology? It is a question that should automatically be on our checklist from time to time – if only to reassure ourselves that our fears are groundless. On the other hand if we sense the possibility of trouble on the horizon, then now is the time to take evasive action.

So I have been looking into my crystal ball. What I see, in the nature of our industry, is inevitably obscured by smoke and dry ice. But I offer a glimpse of my clouded vision of the future as possible food for thought.

What do I see? A lot of healthy growth in the technology – not just in what equipment is supposed to do, but in the reliability with which it does it. This might be disputed by some of my friends who have had unfortunate experiences, but by and large there have been positive improvements in the incidence of such standard syndromes as jammed shutters and amnesia desks. Ergonomics may be variable: there are certainly some machines that offer my fingers little comfort, but the options are wide enough to provide plenty of different keystrokes for different lightfolks.

As to what we do with it? Well the very best of the lighting in all areas is just great. The best is super, but it is the tip of an iceberg: there is, I believe, considerable cause to ponder about the rest. Why do I sometimes seem to have to strain when I should be able to take visibility for granted? And why, when visibility is not a problem, is the light so often rather bland? On the one hand, a light that is so highly dramatic that it defies anyone to suggest that it might not be art; on the other hand, a light whose contrasts are so gentle and its fill so smooth that it seems to be intended for the camera lens rather than the human eye.

Of one thing you can be reasonably certain: such problems are rarely caused by lack of sufficient equipment. It may not all be hanging in the best place, pointed in the right direction, adjusted properly, coloured appropriately or balanced wisely ... but there is usually plenty of it. Perhaps too much. I certainly know that the bulk of my own disasters have tended to be when I was over equipped. One of the first lessons any lighting designer learns is that if there is a visibility hole, the cure is usually not throwing more light at the problem, but a selective checking down of some of the sources already on.

Lighting is all about contrast and balance – a balanced contrast within the picture and a balanced contrast from picture to picture. It is about pace: accelerations and decelerations. Lighting has to be paced towards orgasm. Going at it with a uniform frenzy is a recipe for anticlimax.

This is particularly true of flashing and chasing. Wondrous are the programming possibilities of the machines. The latest spotlights can leap about with choreography so frenetic that it would get St. Vitus excommunicated for laid-back incompetence. But why do so many of those sequences, which I am assured have been precisely programmed, look random?

It is not that the lighting pictures need to be logical. Art is essentially dependent upon illogical decisions. The problem is that so much of what we are offered as lighting statements just does not make visual sense. Certainly not pleasant, rarely stimulating and quite frequently not even provocative. Just boringly meaningless. Alarmingly like lighting attempting to justify the time and money devoted to it.

I can understand how this happens. When I am lighting (and it hasn't changed in the 36 years since I plotted my first professional cue) my desperation does not come from trying to solve technical problems but from the fear that I will not have an idea that is good and appropriate. A fear, alas, quite frequently justified, although occasionally I am lucky enough to bridge the two major potholes on the great lighting design road – too much too soon, and too little too late.

Like most things in life, lighting is all about balancing the desirable and the possible. For a long time, especially in the age of candles and oil, it was the art of the possible – a battle just to get enough light. And many of the control systems of my youth were certainly the art of the possible – indeed when plotting a show, I often felt I was dealing with the art of the impossible. But lighting has increasingly become the art of the desirable. We just have to say what we want and the digital boys in the backroom make it happen.

But it cannot be a clean choice between possible and desirable. There has to be an interaction. The makers have to tell the users what is possible and the users have to tell the makers what is desirable. If there were some way that we could all get a consensus about priorities, profits might go up, blood pressure come down and lighting, especially that in the submerged portion of the iceberg, get better.

That is all part of where I believe the key the future of lighting lies – education. Not so much classrooms, exams, qualifications and certificates, although they all certainly have to be part of it to get people started, particularly for the safety of all concerned. I am more concerned about such fundamentals as the need for everyone to have much more understanding of each other's jobs and problems. Entertainment people generally need to know more about lighting. I always find it much easier to work with directors, designers, performers, managers, whatever, when they know something about what I'm trying to do. Lighting should not be some mysterious mumbo jumbo of chanted numbers … many people are frightened by lighting because its language sounds like a cross between a countdown in mission control and plainsong in a monastery.

My generation grew up in parallel with the great technological surge of the last 30 years. We started to light with a small amount of simple equipment, gradually learning by on-the-job discovery as rigs grew in size and sophistication. In theatre, the advances in technology were paralleled by a general desire to expand the contribution of light to the stage environment.

Our aspirations had clear goals provided by Appia, Craig and the many others who had been frustrated by the technology and attitudes of their time. With the art and the science becoming closely interactive and feeding each other as we juggled the desirable with the possible, the development pace was very quick. Today's young designers are faced with expectations of a higher lighting quality and more complex equipment options for achieving it. Although some problems have gone – particularly the limitations of the control boards of 30 years ago – new lighting designers have to take my generation's point of arrival as their point of departure. And so, before starting, they have to assimilate a considerable amount of the know-how that we acquired experimentally over a long period.

It is not just a simple matter of passing on information although that is a large part of it. Essentially it is about discovery – discovery and debate. I have never been satisfied with what anyone has told me. I need to find out for myself. People have different views and so there is healthy debate, and hopefully we move forward.

What about these mysterious people we call lighting designers? What key aptitudes would seem desirable in a potential professional lighting designer? I would suggest the following: a capacity for strongly imaginative visual thinking; an aptitude for absorbing the possibilities and limitations of various technologies, both new and old, for designing and managing lighting's contribution to performance; an ability to relate to, and work with, the other members of creative and interpretive teams. Articulacy in asking, explaining and discussing.

How do we learn about lighting? Working as part of a lighting team will always be a, probably the, prime learning situation, particularly observation of cause and effect. But how can we prepare people to benefit from this and provide them with a structured learning experience?

I grow daily more convinced that we need a lighting laboratory – an old theatre, or movie house, or redundant church. A grid, lots of equipment of all kinds. A place where groups of lighting people can go at various points in their developing careers for periods of intensive experiment in a structured environment. And not just those people we think of as the users. Let's have the makers too.

Over the past few years, I have been taking staff groups of a well known manufacturer into theatres for weekends. Give salesmen a lighting design problem and a crew – put the factory up one boom and R&D up the other. Send an accountant up the Tallescope, with service and quality control to push it around. Let marketing cut the colours and put them in the frames (the frames that they wrote the spec for). Let the showroom discover that plotting a board for somebody else is not quite the same as demonstrating it to a customer. Swap them all round from time to time. What comes out of it all? Understanding and tolerance of each other, and of the customer. Product modifications. As an investment it is at least self-financing – ask the finance director with his new perspective of the bottom line from the top of the Tallescope. On a raked stage.

Let's have specialist courses for various areas of light. Let's put mixed groups together: rock, Shakespeare, Wagner, disco. Let's get the cross-fertilisation rolling. Our industry needs this laboratory. How about it, PLASA?

Things are looking OK at the moment. But the signs are flickering, flashing – yeah chasing – that lighting may subside into that terminal frenzy of technology which started this little ponder of mine. It need not. It will not. Not if we take evasive action. If we don't, well everything is fine for the moment, but I think I detect some writing on the wall.

Candle Handel (2009)

Storm and tempest raged through the foyers of Karlsruhe Opera House as the audience tried their hand at working the 18th century wind, rain and thunder machines in an exhibition supporting a production of Handel's Radamisto that sought to recreate the acting and technology of baroque staging. The exhibition featured ten European theatres with surviving machinery for scene changing by simultaneous substitution of sets of perspective flats slotted through the floor into understage carriages.

Performances using the old scenes and machines in these theatres are a feature of the summer festival trail, but Karlsruhe Staatstheater is a long way from the baroque idea of a theatre. Built in 1975, it has an asymmetric auditorium and a revolve with three concentric circles

Handel by candlelight

incorporating elevators. However, the concrete of such a house allows a crucial feature of baroque staging that is impossible within the timber fragility of historic houses: real flaming candles are permissible.

In little more than a decade, Handel opera has gone from rarity to mainstream in a box office surge led by the rediscovery of gut strings, keyless woodwind and valveless brass played with minimum vibrato to produce a sound that is particularly apt for the dance rhythms at the heart of Handel's music.

With the dramatic content of his operas having so much contemporary relevance, productions tend to be set in today's world or in a recent period that is significant for the plot. Director's concepts rarely pay even lip service to the original stage directions. However, a 2006 Karlsruhe production of Handel's *Lothario* experimented with setting each act in a different period – Act I in the medieval world of the story, Act II in the baroque of its composition and Act III in the today of the performance. With eighteenth century costumes, sliding wings, and light from real candle flames, it was Act II that reinforced rather than blunted the universality of the story.

This year, for the 250 centenary of Handel's death, Karlsruhe extended period reconstruction to an entire opera. Each of Radamisto's three acts was given the three sets as specified in the wordbook for the 1720 premiére at the King's Theatre in the Haymarket. (All nine model boxes were on foyer display.) Scene changes were effected by sliding wings, with sky and architectural borders alternating between the exteriors and interiors. In the absence of understage machinery, the wings were tracked from above. The means may be different but the effect is the same – although lacking the rumbling sounds that accompany baroque stage machinery.

Wings flickered from the candle poles in each bay, and the characteristic uplight from the floats provided crucial facelight in support of the three pairs of chandeliers – midstage, downstage and over the pit. After some of the Monday morning run-ins I had with fire officers in my stage management days, I never thought I would live to see an opera orchestra playing with 40 guttering candles suspended above them. Although all the flames were in glass chimneys, I'll bet the risk assessment was especially rigorous!

In old theatres, apart from fire risk, the oxygen used up by flames plus their smoke, smell and fumes contributed to an atmosphere that was in no way environmentally friendly – especially as cheaper tallow candles were generally used as an alternative to the more expensive wax. No such problem with quality candles in the efficient air conditioning of concrete Karlsruhe.

It took surprisingly little time to become accustomed to a light so totally different from today's norm. Eye muscles opened their irises very quickly to accommodate low intensity levels, and the gently flickering quality enhanced the painted perspective of the sets while generating an atmospheric chiaroscuro that made the wild extravagance of the baroque costumes appear quite natural. Sets, costumes and lights provided a context in which the formality of the period gestures seemed to be absolutely natural. The crucial footlighting required the singers to play downstage but ten dancers and lots of extras ensured that the stage was always filled with supportive action. Between the vocal sections of arias, Handel opera has extended orchestral ritornelli during which director Sigrid T'Hooft, in a very successful reversal of modern staging practice, often kept the soloist static while regrouping the onlookers.

The formality of the acting style even brought credibility to the very short battle scenes, no longer than two or three thrusts and parries, which so often raise a giggle in modern productions.

Every great work requires fresh interpretation but, from time to time, it is surely important to attempt a revival of the original intentions of writer and composer. In the way that the period instrument revival has informed the playing of old music by modern orchestras, productions using historic staging can provide a stimulus to advance the use we make of our modern technology.

3 LOOKING AT LIGHT

Looking at Light in Nature

Outside

- Sources, natural and artificial.
- Directional quality, whether straight from source or channelled through structures such as trees or buildings.
- Effect of any filtering, e.g. passing through foliage or mist, on texture and colour.
- Colour of light source.
- Colour of reflective surfaces
- Resultant colour of reflected light.
- Effect of direct light on environment surfaces.
- Effect of indirect light on environment surfaces.

Inside

- Externally sourced light penetrating through windows, doors, etc.
- Directional quality of externally sourced light, including consequence of channelling through doors, windows, etc.
- Effect of reflective surfaces in distributing this externally sourced light.
- Internal artificial light sources.
- Directional quality of internal artificial light arising from position of source.
- Colour of light from external and internal sources.
- Colour of reflective surfaces.
- Resultant colour of reflected light.

Looking at light in Paintings and Photographs

- Apparent light sources, natural and artificial.
- Direction in the light quality, whether or not sources are included.
- Colour of light from sources.
- Colour of reflective surfaces.
- Resultant colour of reflected light.
- Effect of direct and indirect light on surfaces.

- Extent to which contrasts of light and shade may have been strengthened to increase the illusion of depth by three-dimensional modelling.

Looking at Light in Film and Video

- Apparent light sources, natural and artificial.
- Directional feel to the light, whether or not source is included.
- Use of contrasts of light and shade to increase the illusion of picture depth and the three-dimensional modelling of objects and people within the picture.
- Use of contrasts of colour to separate actor from environment and increase the illusion of picture depth.

Looking at Light on Stage

- Adequacy of sculptural visibility
- Balance of light levels between individual actors.
- Balance of light between individual items of scenery.
- Balance of light between actors and scenery.
- Use of light to focus audience attention.
- Use of light and shade to create atmosphere.
- Use of colour to create atmosphere.
- Light changes that are obvious to the audience.
- Light changes that the audience is not consciously aware of.
- Extent to which the light appears to be motivated by natural or artificial sources
- Extent to which the light appears to be motivated by directional sources which are not identified with natural or artificial light.
- Any shadows which distract because they are illogical.
- Any light which is visually disturbing.
- Any use of a break-up texture in the light.
- Consequences, good and bad, of light reflecting off surfaces, particularly the floor.
- Any effects, including projection.
- Any use of followspots.
- Any use of dynamically moving beams.
- Consistency in the way in which light is used throughout the production.

Analysing Lighting when not involved in the production

- Did the light fully support the production?
- Was the light fully integrated? – And consistent in its style?
- With its priorities right?
- And its colours?
- Did we always see the actors as clearly as we would have wished and were they sufficiently well sculpted?
- Was the scenery enhanced by the light?
- Well sculpted – or flattened?
- Its mechanics disguised – or exposed?
- Was the light too naturalistic?
- Or should it have been more naturalistic?
- Could the light have contributed more to the atmosphere?
- Should the acting areas have been more tightly selected?
- If automated spotlights were used, did they make a contribution that would have been difficult or impossible with conventional equipment?

Not knowing the background to the production. one might look around to consider:

- How good do the FOH lighting positions appear to be?
- Do the scenery and masking seem to be blocking of potentially useful light positions?

and speculate on:

- How close does the result resemble what the production team set out to achieve?
- Are there indications of compromise?
- If so, do we suspect lack of equipment?
- Or perhaps too much equipment?
- Or insufficient time?
- If we had been lighting designer, would we have wished to do differently?
- If so, would it have integrated with the rest of the production?
- Or would we have wished to alter that also?

Analysing Lighting – When involved with the production

- Did the light support the production as fully as we hoped?
- How closely did the final result match what we set out to achieve?
- Were we flexible in responding to changing ideas as rehearsals developed, and in adapting our plans rather than stick too rigidly with the original concept?
- Did the palette of focused lights provide everything the production team hoped for?
- Was there more compromise than anticipated due to equipment or lack of time?
- Did any lack of time arise from:
- Insufficient allocated lighting time
- Trying to use too much equipment?
- Poorly maintained equipment?
- Knock-on consequences of problems in other areas?
- Were any problems caused by poor FOH lighting positions?
- And did we make the best use of the available FOH positions?
- Was each instrument able to do its planned job or did scenery or masking get in the way? If so, should our planning have been able to anticipate?
- Were automated spotlights available?
- If used, did they contribute positively to lighting quality and/or lighting management?
- If not used, might they have helped lighting quality and/or lighting management?
- Was the lighting style appropriate and consistent?
- Was it fully integrated?
- With its priorities right?
- Was it too naturalistic or should it have been more naturalistic?
- Could it have contributed more to the atmosphere?
- Was the choice of colour filters atmospherically supportive and did they enhance the scenery and costumes?
- Was the scenery generally enhanced by the light?
- Well sculpted – or flattened?
- With its mechanics disguised – or exposed?
- Should the acting areas have been more tightly selected?
- Did we always see the actors as clearly as we would have wished and were they sufficiently well sculpted?
- Given a second chance, would we change the concept or its implementation?

4 THE LIGHTING DESIGN PROCESS

The organisers of the 2004 World Light Fair in Japan made this transcript of my keynote address. It summarises the talks about the stage lighting process that I gave on countless occasions around the world during the previous 40 years.

My presentation today has no pictures. I am afraid it is just words, it is just talk, because

Addressing the 2004 World Light Fair in Japan

things I want to say are about light, not about technology. So pictures won't help as it's about a work process. After about 50 minutes or so, we'll take a short break and then come back for the second part. And, hopefully, some time for questions, which I hope that you will ask me.

It is a really great pleasure for me to come to the World Lighting Fair – to meet old friends and make new ones – I've been doing it all day so far, old friends I haven't seen for years and new friends I've made. Wonderful. And, as I walk around the fair tomorrow, do please come up to me and say hello Francis. Don't say hello Mr Reid. I never recognise Mr. Reid, I never hear this, nobody calls me Mr. Reid. I am Francis. Say, hello, Francis and ask me any questions you may have.

As you are about to discover, my knowledge of technology is rather limited. The core skills of a light designer are handling visual ideas, and handling people. Lighting involves art and technology. It is a kind of marriage of art and technology. But essentially theatre is a people industry. Every morning, every morning of my life before I go to work, as I get out of bed, I say three times, "theatre is a people industry, theatre is a people industry, theatre is a people Industry," and I tell all my students to do this also. It's important. It's people, people, people.

Technology is very important, Very Important, but it is only a tool. Technology provides the technical means which enable ideas to be realised. And using technology is the easiest part of the lighting designers job. The wonders of the new technologies, particularly microprocessing, have ensured that the technical aspects of being a lighting designer have become much easier and easier, with each year of my 50 years doing the job. The hard part of the job is having ideas. Ideas that will support the performers, ideas that will support the words, ideas that will support the music. I find this visual thinking – thinking pictures – I find the visual imagination just as difficult as it was 50 years ago.

Indeed, perhaps it is even more difficult now, because the new technology has given us new possibilities. New technology presents a challenge. New technology provides so many possibilities that we need to be increasingly disciplined. It is very tempting, very tempting, to use a new piece of equipment or a new effect just because it exists.

But we have to exercise considerable self-discipline to ensure that we only use the technological possibilities in the service of the performers – assisting the performers to communicate their interpretation of the music or the words with the audience. I admit to sometimes using a piece of technology just because it is there, and I shouldn't. I try to stop myself doing it. Everything must be in the service of the performance.

I believe very strongly that a lighting designer is not – is not – a light person who works in theatre. A lighting designer is a theatre person who works with light. A theatre person who happens to specialise in light, but remains fascinated by and involved in the whole business – the whole process – of stage performance. The basic requirement for being a lighting designer is a passion for theatre and a fascination with light. Lighting designers are ideas people. But, in the spirit of creative teamwork, they do not impose these ideas, they initiate, they propose, they lead.

Lighting designers are also management people, who plan and monitor a complex sequence of resource intensive procedures involving people and equipment. Staging a performance is a team effort. The ideas of each member: the director, choreographer, scene designer, costume designer, lighting designer, sound designer. All stimulating each other plus, of course, the writer and the composer if it is new, previously unperformed, work.

So, what is the contribution to the team, what is the contribution of the lighting designer? Well, an accurate, if superficial, summary might be that lighting designers take the lead, working with the rest of the

Talking light in Pakistan

production team, in the concept and development of the lighting style – that is, the role that lighting will play in the production. They establish where light is required and where light is not required. Its quality, its colour, its quantity, its brightness, and the direction at which it hits the performers, or their scenic environment.

Then, lighting designers devise a means of implementing this, with decisions about positioning the light instruments, their focus, which type of instrument, which colour filter, and so on.

Then, the lighting designer supervises all the preparation, in association with colleagues who have technical responsibilities. Lighting designers visit the rehearsal room a lot to absorb the action, continue discussions with the director, and the other members of the team. The proportion of the time planning to the time spent working with light on the stage is like – it is the same as – an iceberg. An iceberg has about 20% of the ice visible above the sea, and 80% under the water. Lighting design proportions are similar, only 20% of the work is in the theatre, with 80% preparation: discussion time, drawing time, and most important of all, thinking time. A lot of my decisions are made looking out the window, at the sky, just thinking.

Then, on the stage, the lighting designer implements the design during lighting rehearsals, technical rehearsals and dress rehearsals. According to the prepared plan, but keeping a very flexible approach to possible changes and to any developments all the way through rehearsals.

Now, that was a summary. Let's look at the details. The process for each individual production is never quite the same. Obviously, there will be differences according to such matters as whether the performance is spoken, sung, danced, or all of these things. Whether it is to be played every night for several weeks, months, or even years. There is a show running in London that has been running now for 52 years. (The same play – I have never seen it.) Whether it is a fully scripted show, or maybe it is a showcase for a star personality. The type of venue. All these factors. But even within such factors, the process is different each and every time.

It depends on the personalities of the various team members and the way these people interact. In particular, I find that I work in a different way with each director, depending on such factors as their attitude to lighting, their knowledge of lighting, whether we have worked together before, etc.

Lighting any show involves embarking on a voyage of discovery. The surprises that await even the most experienced light designer are just an inevitable part of any process which involves having ideas and turning those ideas into reality. Even if it were possible to visualise an exact pictorial composition for each moment of the performance, any production is in a constant state of development throughout its rehearsals. This is particularly intensive during the phase when the actors move out of the rehearsal room on to the stage where working in light not only stimulates the light designer's visual thinking – but it triggers ideas in the director, the choreographer and the scenery designer.

This period of working with light is intensively creative, but always short. Its success depends on two major factors. Detailed design work to prepare a palette of lights which will meet all foreseeable requirements, yet offer scope for responding to the unknown idea that we have. And we have to approach stage rehearsals in a spirit of flexibility, in which the lighting designer and the other members of the team respond to the visual stimulation – the visual stimulation of observing the light on the actor and on the scenery.

I said a moment ago that lighting a show is embarking on a voyage of discovery. The planning stage of the design provides a chart for the

British Council lighting course in London

voyage. The planning must ensure the certainty of fail-safe arrival, but provide scope for an imaginative response to discoveries made in the course of integrating the light with all the other elements of the production. The planning has to be planned within agreed budgets and schedules. This is crucial.

Let me tell you a little story about when I was a young lighting designer, many, many, many years ago. Stage scenery is not soundproof. Many years ago I was on one side of a piece of scenery and the manager and the director were on the other side. They could not see me, but I could hear them. The manager said: "Have you worked with Francis before?" And the director replied: "No, this is the first time, but it seems to be going fine." Then, the manager said: "Oh, we use Francis a lot. His lighting is not bad at all. Probably not in the very top category, but it is OK. And, above all, he brings the show in on schedule, within budget and he keeps smiling." So, I built a career on being on schedule, within budget, and keeping smiling. That is how I got my jobs.

Keeping to schedule entails detailed planning with time assessment being pessimistic, not optimistic. An unscheduled 30 minutes on focusing can reduce rehearsal time for the performers and can incur additional technical costs, not just for the lighting technicians but for all the people who are standing by to use the stage.

The key importance of advance planning is to ensure that the maximum proportion of allotted lighting time is available for creative exploration. This cannot be over emphasised. On several occasions, I have been asked if it would help to have more money for equipment. My reply has usually been that I would rather have more time to make better use of the equipment that we already have.

Although the details of the work in process differ according to the membership of the individual production team, there is a basic sequence of decisions that a lighting designer has to make. So let us now follow that decision sequence from first reading the words or hearing the music until the first performance. Each lighting designer develops their own personal version of this process, but there are a number of broad decision areas with one decision tending to lead to another in a fairly logical sequence. And self-questioning is central to these decisions.

My first reading – let's start with a spoken drama, a play – begins with a study of the words. Every aspect of the production must grow out of the words or the music. My first reading is quite fast. I approach the script like a novel – just a story – to get a feel for the overall shape, the story line, the characters. I try to think as little as possible about light. Just get to know the play, the words.

My second reading is very, very slow. It takes a long time. I mark the text using coloured highlight pens. In one colour, I mark any mention of light in the text or in the author's stage directions. In a different colour I mark any words in the text that trigger a lighting idea in my mind. I make notes of such matters as locations of scenes, changes in time, changes in emotion – particularly happiness, sadness and special effects. And when music forms an integral part of the work, my study of the words will be followed immediately by immersion in the music score. Indeed, listening to an opera is likely to come before reading the words. For classical ballet or modern dance, music has to be the starting point, since any written material will be restricted to an outline scenario. Maybe the work has no story line, it will have nothing at all if it is an abstract piece, only the music.

Now, few lighting designers can read a music score to the extent of looking at the printed notes and hearing them clearly in their head. I cannot. However, I can find my way around a written score, following the notes while I listen to the music. So, I can make notes in the music. For revivals of old shows, commercial recordings are usually available, and for new shows there is usually a demo disk, possibly with just a piano and some singers to attract the sponsors and the backers. To absorb and familiarise the music, I just play it as background to any routine work that I am doing. In my house, everybody knows the music for the next show because it is playing all the time.

So, I am concentrating on a familiarisation with the music and I am responding to the atmosphere that it seems to be creating. My aim during the first study process is just to get to know the words and music. I have some thoughts, some emotional responses, some ideas, but I try to keep an open mind until I have met the rest of the team. At this early point, I do not research any background to the piece – period or anything. And, I never look at photographs of old productions of the show. All that comes later.

So, these preliminary studies prepare the light designer for discussion with the rest of the production team. Discussion which will evolve the style in which the team approaches the production.

How early should the light designer be involved in planning? It varies according to many factors, including the people involved. Some productions are in a classic established style, a style that is almost ritualistic. A style that the teams are familiar with. Styles like this require less discussion than a style that is attempting a fresh approach.

It is not easy to identify a universal best time, but you can identify the last possible moment. Although I hope it is never as late as this, the last possible time for the light designer to be involved is just before the scene designs are given final approval and sent to the workshops for building. At this point, the lighting designer can often identify an adjustment that will help the lighting, an adjustment that the scenery designer will be happy with, an adjustment that can be made to the cardboard scene model with a knife at no cost, but would be very expensive to make after all the scenery is built.

My earliest ever involvement for a new musical was an opera. I met the composer more than a year before rehearsals began, and before he orchestrated it. He was very interested in light. He played it on the piano to me and sang it, and made some cuts and wrote some extra music in the places where I wanted them for lighting changes. But that was exceptional.

Normally, my own preferred moment is when the director and scenery designer already have had some discussions and the design is beginning to emerge. The light designer is usually the first person with whom the director and the scenery designer share their ideas. This can put a lot of responsibility on the lighting designer. So I have to proceed with considerable delicacy and tact, especially if I am not very happy with their concept. The light designer, at this moment, has to be positive. I try to avoid using the word problem. It is time to be positive and cheerful.

But, at this time, the foremost question in the lighting designer's mind is what is the role of lighting going to be in this production. I go to the discussions with some knowledge of the piece and some ideas. But as I have said, I go with an open mind.

Let's just take a moment to consider the possibilities of light's contribution to any performances. The fundamental requirement is obviously to illuminate the actors so that they are visible to the audience. If any actor is not fully visible at a particular moment, this should be the result of a deliberate decision taken for dramatic effect. It should not happen by default. The precise nature of the illumination will vary according to the type of performances. Faces in a spoken play, particularly eyes, are very important for character projection. You need to see the eyes of a speaking actor. However, in more physical forms of theatre, especially dance, full illumination of the body is of prime importance. The light that reveals should also sculpt. So, we need to choose angles that will enhance the three dimensional, sculptural quality of the actors and their scenery.

Now, light inevitably imposes some degree of selectivity upon audience vision, and it influences the atmosphere.

The director in film and television has exact control of what the audience looks at, by cutting between cameras, by zooming in and out, but in theatre all of the audience look at all of the stage all of the time. So, light provides an important way for the director to focus audience attention on certain parts of the stage action.

Another possible major use of light is to create atmosphere, whether created by contrasting light and shade, or by colour. Selectivity and atmosphere can be delicately, or broadly indicated.

I saw a play last week. I know the lighting operator. And, after the play I said to her: "Well, you had an easy night tonight. Only two or three lighting changes." And she said to me: "There were 245 cues, I did 245 lighting changes." Now, just because I had not consciously noticed these changes does not mean they were wasted. They were very subtly working on my sub-conscious, and helping the actors to convey the intention of the writer and the director. There's a lot of sub-conscious light changes you don't see.

A further major influence on lighting style is the extent to which the light on the stage relates to natural and artificial light. Does the light appear to be motivated by natural sources, the sun and the moon, or artificial lighting fixtures?

Most dramas are about real people, their problems, loves, fears, relationships, but the scenery in today's theatre is frequently symbolic, often metaphorical, not realistic at all. So the light often has to form a bridge between realistic people and non-realistic scenery.

At this point the prime decision area in lighting design is finding a credible answer to the question: what contribution will light make to this production. The answer will almost certainly include sculptural visibility. It may involve selection of areas and atmosphere in all sorts of ways, it may well involve special effects, and it will certainly need to consider the extent that it conforms with the behaviour of light in nature.

Returning to that first meeting with the scene designer and director, the search for style leads me to think about such matters as how naturalistic, how selective, how atmospheric, how softly diffuse, how sculptural, how coloured, any projections, any special effects? These kinds of questions.

Now, if you ask these directly to a director, they tend to be conversation stoppers. So you have to tease the answers out gently. This is difficult. You have got to tease, you have got to ask questions to find out. For example, when the director, or the scene designer talk about dark, are we sure they mean low intensity, low brightness, or do they mean a deeply deeply saturated dark colour. Only careful cross-questioning will find you the answers. At the first meeting with the director and the scene designer, I often feel that my job is like being a detective.

I usually leave this first meeting with some disconnected ideas buzzing around in my head, although still searching for a clear vision of the production and its lighting. The meeting may stimulate some research in background areas – historical, geographical, sociological, architectural, literary – particularly if the show is a musical made out of a play or a novel. You are quite likely to find me in a museum or a library.

As a consensus begins to emerge about an approach to the production in general and the lighting in particular, the light designer looks for any details of the scenery model that could conflict with the proposed use of light. How reflective is the floor? A glossy floor can look wonderful and provide faces with a flattering soft uplight from below. However, the scatter of reflected light from even a single beam can spoil the dramatic effect of picking out an actor from surrounding darkness. Are there any surfaces of the scene which are likely to collect so much light that they should be painted a darker shade in order to appear on the stage as they do on the model.

Are there any possible minor modifications to the set that the scene designer would be happy with and improve access for light? Is there likely to be any difficulty in lighting faces because large areas of the background scenery are coloured the same tones as the flesh of a face? Scene designers often light their models for me with a single desklamp to produce a dramatic effect such as shining diagonally from the back of the stage through a scenery arch. Very dramatic, but I know that there will have to be light for the actors: so I have to be very tactful and warn them so it doesn't surprise them in the theatre. I tell them now. I say something like: "Oh, that is a lovely effect, a really wonderful effect. Such a pity we will only be able to show it for a few seconds before adding some front light to the actors face, That will inevitably dilute the effect but I will do everything I can to keep that balance of picture.

I need to warn everybody, but I need to keep their confidence. Theatre is a people industry.

Very important for me personally is the very first rehearsal in the rehearsal room. I always try to be there, for two reasons. Firstly, this rehearsal usually begins with reading through the script, or singing through the music, and no matter how many times I have read the script, I always find it comes to life much, much more when I hear it read by actors. So I want to hear them read it. Secondly, it is an opportunity to get to know the actors: performers need to have confidence in their light designer.

Actors can be very nervous about technology. They work for several weeks in the rehearsal room, perfecting their performance, then they bring it to the stage where they only have a very short time, a few days – sometimes just a few hours – to integrate these performances with all the highly technical apparatus of the stage. It is a very scary time for the performers. They come on to the stage for their first dress rehearsal with scenery, costume, music, and lights. Lights which can support their performance, or damage it. Actors know that light can make the young look old, or the beautiful look ugly. So, in the auditorium, they see the lighting designer at the production table with plans, computer screens and talking numbers into a microphone. An actor once said to me: "I often feel at this moment that my performance is going to be taken over by mission control."

So it is important that actors know who their lighting designer is, that he has been attending rehearsals from time to time, and that he is really interested in their show. A good start is when the actors are gathering in the rehearsal room for the very first time. They are standing there, they are drinking tea, coffee, rather nervously. The nerves don't show – they can hide them because they are actors – but they are nervous. So this is a good moment to say hello and make friends. Theatre is a people industry.

Once the production is in rehearsal, the lighting designer visits frequently, observing how the intended use of the set develops as the director works with the actors. This will lead to analysing the use of the set in terms of the style we have agreed.

It is self-questioning. Sitting in the rehearsal room, I ask myself questions as I look at the rehearsal. How does the stage divide into areas that require independent selection by light? Does the size of these areas necessitate further sub-division for practical reasons? How does the stage divide by colour? How many different colours are required for mixing in each of these divisions? Does the colour division correspond to the area division? Which lights are so critical in size, shape and colour of their beams as to require specially focused spotlights rather than spotlights that can double as general acting area lights? Are there any special effects?

The answers to these questions provide the information to start to evolve the lighting plan, usually drawn at a scale of 1:25 or 1:50. This shows the position in which each lighting instrument will be mounted, the type of light of each instrument in each position, any accessories such as gobos and the colour filter number. The drawing board which I used all my working life has been overtaken by the computer screen. We live in a world where the mouse is mightier than the pen. But, whether drawing on screen or on paper, the decisions to be made are the same.

The first marks I put on a plan are the places I need to position lighting instruments in the auditorium or on the stage. It is the direction at which the light strikes the performer, or strikes the piece of scenery, that is the most important factor in all stage lighting. So important that I would rather have an old historic, ancient, dirty spotlight in the correct position than the most wonderful new hallelujah spotlight in the wrong position. So, at first on the plan I make little crosses where light will be and where it will focus. I don't think at this time about whether it is a profile, a Fresnel or whatever.

I go for ideal positions first although there is inevitably some conflict of interest. In the auditorium with the architecture – where you would like to put a light in the auditorium, very often there is no place to mount it. And, on the stage, we often have to compromise with where the scenery is. We have an ideal but some compromise is inevitable.

Then, and only then, do I start to think which would be the ideal type of instrument for each of the chosen positions. This ideal is also followed by compromise according to availability, budgets, priorities. The ideal choice will be based primarily on the quality of light desired, and the amount of control required over the beam size and the beam shape, and this choice will also take into consideration the relative time required to focus simpler or more complex instruments.

The time available for the lighting designer to work on the stage is usually very short. So, I like to save as much time as possible when focusing the lights so that I have more time available for the key phase of creating the lighting pictures.

Parcans are my favourite instrument, up-down, left-right, OK. Or the simple focus spot – the Fresnel – up-down, left-right, big-small, OK. Much quicker to focus that profile spots with two independent lenses and four shutters all interacting.

Automated lights are often called intelligent lights but you'll never hear me call them intelligent lights. I call them obedient lights. Because their wonderful feature is that they do what they are told. They do what the lighting designer tells them. An intelligent light would have a mind of its own, but I want to tell the light what to do, so it is an obedient light. Obedient lights make a strong contribution to lighting management because they need no access for focusing. And they can be refocused many times throughout the show.

The most wonderful thing for me is not that they do all these things, but instead of using a lamp for one special in one moment, I can refocus it continuously through the time of the performance. And, in many forms of theatre this capability of being refocused when they are not lit is even more important than dynamically moving beams. They of course are great, they offer us possibilities I love. I hardly ever use them as you see them in an exhibition. Great in a disco, but I don't do it much on the stage. I love to shift focus, boldly or delicately, from one part of the stage to the other. If the light moves from left to right, it takes the eyes of the audience, sometimes quite slowly.

It is the moving beam that commands the eye of the audience to follow it. I love a wide beam that narrows as the attention goes on a single actor. I love the way you can accelerate and slow down the movement. Or, you can start slow and accelerate. The wonderful things you can do with the clean continuous movement of a single beam rather than the old way we had to do it with sequential fades: having a lot of multiple beams and cross fading them. A wider beam to a narrower now all done in one clean movement.

Our future surely includes ever increasing use of these obedient lights. It is going to be great although, alas, not for me – I am too old, my lighting days are finished. However all you young people are going to have a great time with the obedient light, it does wonderful things. I can refocus it, I can change the gobos, I can have unlimited colour, it is wonderful there, in the first scene. But in the second scene, I don't want it there, I want it here. So the future I see has the moving lights tracking along the trusses, because the most important feature of light is the angle it hits the performer at.

So, instrument choice usually has less compromise, but there are questions. How far does the available equipment match the ideal requirements? If some of the instruments that are available are not exactly ideal, are they sufficiently close for an acceptable compromise? How can we make the most cost effective use of the rental budget? Beside my drawing board and computer is the all essential pocket calculator with the budget so that I can do a minus sum every time I use a light from rental.

The next decision is the hardest for me: choice of filter. Although a wide range of filters may be used on the scenery, the colour for most of the acting areas in each production is a relatively small group that you need to discover. The choice is narrowed down in two steps. You go for hue, the basic spectrum divided into red, orange, blue, whatever. Then, saturation, the variation from pale to deep, and then there are a further two steps which arise from the pigment in the scenery paint, the costumes and the make-up. Do we need blues with a high red or green content? Ambers of varying proportion of orange and yellow? Then the filter numbers.

I have always in my pocket, a swatch book and a Maglite. I am never without them. I shine the Maglite through the filter at the paint on the model, or at the actors skin or at the costume fabrics. You have to do it particularly with costumes, because although you see a design, creative interpretation of making a costume involves the choice of materials, possible dyeing or painting the fabrics, adding trimmings, etc, etc, all of which can affect the filter choice.

Lighting designers devote a lot of their lives to considering priorities. At each phase of the process, first assessment of the requirement usually seems to be irreconcilable with budget, finance and scheduled time, but continually examination and re-examination to determine priorities enables an apparently minimum number to be reduced even further.

Determining priorities is hard time consuming work but I find that it often leads to better lighting. This is bad news if you are selling lighting equipment but I find that the less equipment I use the lighting is usually cleaner and better.

So, we arrive at this major document of the light design, the scale plan, showing the location of each instrument, its precise type, its accessories, gobos, irises, filter numbers, control channel numbers and some indication of focus.

The lighting plan is supported by a whole series of schedules: detailed focus information for each instrument, a patching schedule if the channel numbers differ from the dimmer socket numbers, all the instruments and accessories all the rigging equipment, including the cable, equipment on rental, colour call showing the number of pieces of each size of each filter.

For most of my life, compiling these schedules was hard work, but one of the joys of computer aided design is that the computer makes these lists at a stroke of a key. Several software programs produce every conceivable piece of lighting paperwork, on a personal computer. The capability includes tracking sheets to record the level of every channel in every cue. Programs such as WYSIWYG, an acronym for What-You-See-Is-What-You-Get, allow lighting plans to be drawn on a computer screen, and software that generates all the necessary schedules when requested by a few simple keystrokes.

The final indispensable document is the cue-synopsis, which should be developed by the light designer in the rehearsal room and agreed with director, choreographer, set designer, and the member of the stage management team who will be calling the cues. A cue synopsis should list the cue number, the up and down timings in seconds for incoming and outgoing memories, the position in the script, and the cue intention: a brief description of what is intended to happen on each cue.

I find that the easiest way to arrive at a consensus is to prepare this list and circulate it to all members of the production team. Theatre people, I find in general, are frightened of a blank sheet of paper. Ask them to write down their ideas, and their writing hand becomes paralysed. But, write your own ideas on the paper, and they are happy to edit them.

The plan that was the lighting designer's principal worksurface now becomes the major communication document. It carries all the essential information required by the technicians for rigging and it gives the set designer, the stage manager and stage crew a clear confirmation of the space allocated to lighting, bars, trusses, booms, ladders, stands. Once the plan copies have been distributed, and the recipients have had an opportunity to examine them, the lighting designer should ask about problems. You ask, not wait to be told. And, of course, any subsequent changes have to be notified to anyone likely to be affected, even in the most minor way.

Scenery, costumers, prop designs are small scale models or drawings of what will actually appear on the stage. But, the graphics of lighting design bear no pictorial relation to the stage lighting intentions that they convey. So lighting is the most difficult part of a theatre production to indicate in advance.

Consequently, when a production moves from the rehearsal room onto the stage, less is known of the lighting designer's intentions than of any other members of the team. This is rather frightening for the rest of the production team. It is frightening for the actors, and it is frightening for the lighting designer.

I see the last run-through in the rehearsal room, and the action is very clear. Maybe they are using the sound effects tapes. They have tried the costumes to see that they fit, maybe the director has seen the scenery in the workshops. Everything is known about the show, except the lighting, because the lighting plan is just a plan of how the equipment will be hung. It doesn't actually show you the picture. So it is a very frightening moment for everybody.

We have reached the point where the move is made from the rehearsal room onto the stage. So I think this might be a good place to take a ten minute break for people who want to stretch their legs, or smoke, or whatever, and then we'll talk about what happens on the stage.

Intermission

The major purpose of all the design work, that 80% of the iceberg under the sea, is so that when we get into the theatre is every minute of stage time can be used to maximum advantage. It is always short. If it isn't short in Japan, then it is the only country in the world that it's not short of time. Everywhere I go there is a time problem – a big one.

When we get onto the stage the key creative phases in this process will be the focusing and the plotting. But, before they can be started, all the lights have to be rigged and the scenery positioned.

The standard for a good lighting design plan is that it should carry all the necessary information for all the equipment to be rigged. It should carry all this information so clearly, that the lighting designer does not need to be present during the rigging process, just arrive in time to focus and have no surprises.

However, although I don't want to interfere in any way with the technicians work, I personally like to be present in the theatre while the lights and scenery are being hung. Despite detailed planning, there can still be unforeseen problems. No matter how accurate the scale model, the scenery is multiplied by a factor of 25 during its realisation in the workshops. When a model is scaled-up by 25, there can always be a few visual surprises. So, if problems arise, I am there to solve them.

As everything gradually comes together, I can walk about the stage, and check that my calculations are OK. That the light that I put there will actually hit this part of the stage, that its beam won't be blocked by some piece of scenery. Also, as the technicians flash out the lights to check that they are working OK, I can see how the scene painting reacts to my filters. On several occasions in my life, the light from an unfocused spotlight just being checked has hit a piece of scenery in a way that gave me some wonderful new idea that I never imagined before. But, most of all I just absorb the atmosphere, and become slowly acquainted with the scale of the scenery. It is an exciting time.

Once the rigging is complete, I like to make the final check myself, calling for the channels, one by one, just to make absolutely sure that everything is plugged according to my plan – that I have got the right bit of paper. The confusion that can arise from one or two wrong numbers on a plan can waste a lot of time later during the focusing. Although lighting plans are normally drawn to a scale of 1:25, I normally like to use a 1:50 reduction when focusing. A smaller sheet of paper is much easier to handle, as I walk about.

Although detailed design work has resulted in each light having a clearly allocated function, the actual focusing process is a time of intense creativity. It is a time when lighting designers remain flexible, ready to react to any unforeseen opportunity yet aware, in the back of their mind, of the possibility of any knock-on consequences of making a change. Very careful, you have to be.

As I have said, the way that an unfocused light beam accidentally strikes a piece of scenery when the instrument is first switched on triggers an idea, not just in the light designer It could be that the director happens to be in the theatre, or the scene designer, and they get a new idea. You never know where the good ideas come from. Some of the good lighting ideas come from me, some from the director. I also give my ideas to the director on non-lighting things. We are a team working together.

Under ideal conditions, the scenery will be complete and all the furniture and the decorations. Everything will be quiet to allow the light designer and technicians to concentrate. But often – well, it is not really often, it is normal – there will be some noise and even a little chaos as the finishing adjustments are put to the scenery, and its paintwork. Maybe not in Japan, but certainly in England, scenery often comes on to the stage not quite finished, and the painters come and they want to complete while we work. At worst, the scenic preparations could be so behind schedule, that voices have to compete with power tools. On the few occasions when I have ideal focusing conditions, the piano tuner has arrived. The possibility of noise during focusing is yet another reason for good advanced planning.

The tried and tested way of focusing is for the lighting designer to stand in the centre of the beam, with back to the light, giving instructions by word and gesture to the technician who is adjusting the light.

Normally, when focusing, I am on the stage, and want to have light focused for me here. I stand in the light with my back to it. The light does not shine in my eyes and if I can see a full shadow of myself, I know I will be lit. Most of the time, I have to think a little bit like this, (hand above head) because my actors always seem to be taller than I am. I use gestures and you can do this against the noise. Unless of course you have obedient lights, then you just need to talk to the lights through their programmer.

This way I can check the light for the actor and also see the effect of the beam, especially its edge on the scenery. (Facing into the light you don't see what the light is doing to the scenery.) It is important to give instructions in a clear, cheerful and encouraging voice.

To ensure that we know exactly what light is coming from which particular source, it is best to have only one spot on at a time, and then you know that any light must be from that spotlight. Unless, of course, we are checking the overlapping join with another spotlight.

I find it surprising how much time can be saved if, as a matter of routine, the next light is switched on before the previous one is switched off, so the stage never goes completely black. It is also much safer. The whole process is quicker and easier when the light designer gives simple instructions. Up-down, left-right, big-small, harder-softer, shutter the sides in, accompanying the words with these simple gestures.

Key aims in focusing are to ensure that an actor will be lit everywhere in the area which has been allocated to that particular instrument and the only way to be certain is for the light designer to move about in the beam. The centre of the beam is kept at face level taking particular care when working with simple spots, particularly Fresnels, to keep the centre high before adjusting the barn doors. The light beams of adjoining areas are overlapped smoothly, both to the left-right and upstage-downstage, trying to make the beam edges and the actor light hit the scenery in an unobtrusive way. Normally, using a soft edge which will not show on the actors face or scenery as a line. An edge on the scenery can often be disguised by coinciding with a feature of the scenery structure or the scenery decoration. Hard edges make such a positive visual statement, pulling the audience eye, that the brain, usually sub-consciously, tries to find a logic for the edge. Edges should only be hard for a definite purpose otherwise, it is soft. I doubt if I use, in an average show, more than 5% of the lights with hard edges.

When the focusing is complete, we can begin to compose the lighting pictures. In Britain, we call this plotting, but the Canadian term, level setting, captures the essence of what actually happens. Deciding which channels are alight, and their intensity levels.

It is of course perfectly feasible to program all the cues on a laptop away from the theatre and then download them into the theatre's control system prior to running through and making adjustments in conjunction with the rest of the production team. But, I can't do that. It is a viable method, but it just doesn't work for me. I know a lot of people can do it. But doesn't work for me.

Lighting for me is a painting process. I need to see the effect of the beam. As each beam is added to the picture, I want to see the effect. I don't know in advance exactly which spotlights I will use on a particular scene. The lighting instruments that I hang and focus are to provide a palette of light beams that I know I will need. The painter has a palette of colours, I have a palette of light beams. I need to see them building and mixing. But this is only personal. I know that some people can prepare wonderful lighting on their laptops in their hotel room. Not me.

Actors are not present at a traditional plotting rehearsal, but it is often useful to have a couple of people, often junior members of the stage management team, who have been at all the rehearsals and so are familiar with the show. They can take up positions in the acting areas as required to see the light on their faces.

When control was by the old manual boards with no memory, alterations at subsequent rehearsals were difficult, so balancing of levels had to be particular accurate at this first light. But, with today's computer memory boards, the overall picture can be composed but the fine balancing of the face lights postponed until later rehearsals with the actors. However, the presence of actors is particularly important in modern dance where there is usually no scenery and the dancers define the space by the way they populate it.

When you are composing lighting pictures, painting with light, the key piece of equipment is the lighting designer's eye. You light with your eye. The lighting designer's eye is supported by the eyes of the director, the choreographer, the set designer, costume designer. All of them have different visual priorities. Hopefully, the light designer will be able to produce a result which incorporates all those specialist priorities. However, some compromise is inevitable from time to time.

At this point, I abandon the big lighting plan, and work from a series of cards. They used to be this size (index card example), but now that I my eyes are old, the cards are bigger. This card, called a magic sheet, which is so personal that only I can read it. The magic sheet is a diagram which gets me very quickly to the numbers for a particular area or colour.

There are occasions, certainly for single performances or very short runs when it maybe convenient, even be desirable, for the designer and the operator to be the same person. But for a sequence of performances in the same venue, it is more appropriate to have a separate operator (or a pair of alternating operators to allow for evenings at home with the family). I certainly want the freedom to concentrate on the stage without having to think about operational procedures. And, at later rehearsals, to be able to move around the auditorium to see how the stage looks from different seats. I also need the freedom to talk during rehearsals with other members of the production team without having to keep an ear open for my cue to operate the next light change.

I have a close relationship with operators. I try to keep them fully involved in what I am trying to do and the reasoning behind some decisions which often may seem strange to them. They are an important second pair of eyes. Looking at the stage from a different angle, often from a level higher than me, they can often see things that I cannot. So they help me. I am much more interested in who the operators are as people rather than the control system that they are operating. I find that if an operator has experience of a control system and likes it – very important that they like – and I explain what I am trying to do, then everything is possible. The operator is more important than the machine.

My other close relationship is with the stage manager who will call the cues, integrating the light changes with the stage action, the scenery movement, the sound effects. The effectiveness of the timing of a light change depends on the interaction between the speed of the change and the moment when it begins.

So now I am sitting at the production table with the members of the production team. All the lights are focused, and before I call for a blackout, I usually say to the operator in the control room: "When I ask you for a channel number, bring it to 70% unless I give you a different level." This is because I try to avoid using 100% levels in the initial plotting of light pictures. I want to have the possibility of fine balancing during subsequent rehearsals. If I use 100% at first, there is no upwards, there is no over drive. I want to be able to go up and down, so I take my maximum as 70%.

There is no absolute light level for the human eye. The human eye is much more flexible in its light requirements than the digital eye of video or the emulsion eye of film. The muscular iris in the human eye opens and closes to adjust for variable brightness levels. So balance is the key to our perception of brightness. Indeed, if I have a scene where the most important actor looks not so bright as the unimportant ones, the answer is often not to increase the light on the important one but to reduce it on the others. It is all in the balance: the balance between individual actors, the balance between elements in the scenic environment, the balance between the actors and the scenery.

I get very nervous before this painting with lights session. Very nervous. Will all my individually focused beam combine to make the pictures that have until now only existed in the imaginations of the production team? I have never conquered the flutter of heart beat, the sinking in the stomach, that comes when I sit down at the production table in the auditorium with the director and the rest of the team. These discussions with the director, the choreographer, the set and costume designer – discussions where we all tried to find words to describe visual things, did we all mean the same thing?

So as I start to build up the first picture from the beams, my ears are twitching for a favourable sound from the rest of the team gathered around me. Maybe I hear an appreciative murmur, even a whispered 'nice', but more often there is just that ominous silence which passes for concentration. I try to interpret any grunts and ums, as I move towards the moment when I say: "How do you feel about something like this for the opening?" Perhaps we make a few adjustments, before we move on. After the first few cues, it becomes much easier. My nagging fears were unfounded: we were talking about the same thing. As the work progresses, some members of the team drift away, content that the lighting seems to be progressing in a style that they are happy with. One director that I worked regularly with would stand up after 20-25 minutes and say: "Please can I go home now? I see from the first pictures, that we all talk of the same thing. I am happy, so if its OK by you, I go to bed, you carry on working and I see it tomorrow."

I find that the light on a scene has two components. Usually, there is a broad statement of light, perhaps a strong directional beam. Perhaps it is the sun, the moon, or just an abstract beam, but a fairly positive pictorial lighting statement, usually coming from the back of the stage, or perhaps the side but not very often from the front. This is the light that the audience are aware of, but there are also lights filling in, usually from the front, so that the performers can project, by making the vital eyes and the mouth visible.

So, I begin by painting in the broad strokes of directional beams, then gradually fill in the actor light and finally these little delicate touches that bring the scene paint to light.

With the rapid memory access of computer control desks, I have an opportunity during the rehearsals to fine-tune the balance on the actors. So, at the light plotting session, I can concentrate on the broader picture, and take particular care to get the timings right.

The timings are particularly crucial, particularly the differential between the relative speed of incoming light and outgoing light. It is never a straight cross-fade: there are accelerations and slowing down and change of speed. I try to get these as correct as possible before we start rehearsing with the actors, because once we are rehearsing with the actors, the light has to coordinate with scene changes, music, sound and actors. So I want to be able to integrate this at an early point.

I find that the plotting of light starts slowly then it gets quicker and quicker as we progress. This is partially because of becoming familiar with the lights as they have been focused, but mostly it is because I am more and more able for many of the cues to use modified versions of the previous one. Cue 78 might be cue 23 plus small additions or subtractions of channels.

Then, comes the rehearsal known as the tech in Britain, when the actors are coordinated with the scenery, lights, everything – all the technology of the stage. Only the orchestral players will be missing; probably just a conductor, keyboards and maybe drums. Most technical rehearsals are long and slow, stopping for each and every problem to be solved. If a show lasts two hours, we would normally allow ten hours for the technical rehearsal because there are so many things to do.

The key areas are the positions of the cues: timing of cues, balance with pictures, and this interlinking between the position and the timing. Every time a cue doesn't look quite right, the answer may be to speed it up, or slow it down, or more likely a changed differential between the up-speed and the down-speed. Or maybe to give the go sooner, or later, or a mixture of both. Fine balances, particularly between areas of relative light intensity on several actors can only really be achieved when they are in position. A balancing that continues until the final rehearsal.

Whereas the performers concentrate on the mechanics at the first rehearsal with light, the dress rehearsals are a time for more acting. In quiet periods the light designer can adjust intensities. But nothing should be done to disturb the flow of the performance, or upset the concentration of the actors, or the concentration of the board operator, or the concentration of the stage manager. Theatre is a people industry.

This is mostly a time for viewing the stage from different angles and making notes for adjustment to be made after the rehearsal. But I have to be aware of making too many adjustments: there comes a point when the apparent solution can cause more problems than it cures.

On the first night, there should be nothing left for the lighting designer to do except try to enjoy the performance and if necessary take notes.

The lighting designer or an assistant should keep an eye on the production from time to time. During the early days of a long run, performances mature and this can involve some minor repositioning of actors. The venue's lighting technicians carry out a daily lamp check, that nothing has blown: no filaments or lamps blown. And, they have regular focus checks, paying particular attention to any spotlight that is likely to be knocked by moving scenery.

Life as a lighting designer spans agony and ecstasy. You go from deep depression to "wonderful!" and back very quickly. The quest for perfection requires a lot of self-assessment and that includes self-doubt. I am rarely happy with more than 80% of my work, and usually much, much less.

But, there are moments of satisfaction. Let me tell you about just one highlight. Perhaps the climax of my career, quite a few years ago now. We had finished a dress rehearsal and the director was giving notes. He went around with his notebook, it was a long session involving deep individual discussions with each of the actors in turn. It was a civilised theatre company: the notes were given in the theatre bar. Finally he got to me. Flicking the pages over one by one, "Francis, Francis," he said. "I am terrible sorry, but 1 didn't notice the lighting tonight." What more could I wish for!

It was a complex light plot,with a mixture of snap changes and delicate fades, but he did not notice them The director did not notice them happening because the light was totally integrated with the acting and all the other aspects of the show. That was the climax of my career, 25 years ago, the peak, downhill ever since.

I am often asked about the personal qualities and aptitudes that would be helpful to a lighting designer. I suggest a committed interest, preferable a passion, for all aspects of performance and visual arts. A determination that puts being a lighting designer before financial security and a scheduled social life. A capacity for strongly imaginative visual thinking, and an aptitude for absorbing the possibilities and the limitations of various technologies old and new: technologies for designing and managing light's contribution to staged performances. An ability to relate to and work with the other member of creative and interpretative teams. Articulacy in asking, explaining, and discussing.

My scores on all but one of these are much lower than I would wish. The exception, the one on which I think I score high is, passion. And, fortunately, that is the most important. Passion will drive you there, with a bit of luck.

That kind of describes what a lighting designer does in general, and what this lighting designer does in particular, but everyone has their variation of it. The technology is wonderful, the technology is great and it is getting better. You just have to go to the exhibition downstairs and see what is possible. But, technology is a tool. You've got your eyes, and you've got your imagination. They are the most fantastic tool box available to you.

5 CONFERENCES AND TRADE SHOWS

ABTT Show 1980

The ABTT Trade Show 80 was, for me, a unique exhibition experience. I am no beginner when it comes to attending the entertainment industry's exhibitions. Paris, Montreux, Karlsruhe, New York, Washington and. Cape Town housed some of the bigger trade fairs which have given me past opportunities of studying the latest hardware.

But last week I was able to go to the ABTT's product bonanza at the Shaftesbury Theatre with a sharper glint in my eye. No window shopping, this time, I was there as a buyer. I was (at least in terms of my little theatre's budget) a big spender.

I was faced with just about the most difficult buying decision that can confront any theatre at the present time: the choice of a new lighting control board.

Lighting controls have achieved detergent status. They come in similar packages and the finer points of their individual advantages are more apparent to their salesmen than to their potential users.

Everyone is making memory controls: some manufacturers are successfully selling them while others are still trying to get in on the act. One admires the marketing man who announced in transatlantic tones of ringing sincerity that he intended to put ten into the UK this year. One admired his confidence but one wondered if he had done his market research.

The swing over to memory controls in the past five years has been so dramatic that the market must be quite close to saturation. Even if a memory desk is written off in seven years, there is a life expectancy of some ten- to 12 years.

So, personally speaking, the chance to flip from one manufacturer's stand to another was an excellent chance to compare and contrast the product that I was buying. But – and it is a big BUT – I sympathise with all those visitors who were muttering about the dominance of lighting exhibits.

In the early days of the ABTT, cynics were in the habit of describing the Association as 'a consortium of electricians, lighting designers and Strand Electric' and it was noted with some scorn that the logo resembled a series of spotlight colour frames.

It is very doubtful if there was ever any truth in this … and the present ABTT is certainly very far from being dominated by the lighting men. Nevertheless, the mystique surrounding the lighting process and the ease with which its hardware can be identified and packaged has led to a competitive expansion which must surely benefit theatres more than shareholders. Definitely an area in which industrial sponsorship of theatre is actively at work!

It was perhaps inevitable that the ABTT award for technical innovation went to a lighting device. CCT, who revolutionised profile spots in the 70s, have now applied fresh clear clean thinking to remote colour changing and it is now obvious that it is to John Schwiller's CCT research team that we must look for likely breakthroughs in luminaires.

Rank Strand will obviously do themselves a great deal of short-term good in European markets by their rediscovery of the simple plano-convex focus spot – long discarded by Anglo-American lighting design. But for the long-term future of lights. I will continue to pin my personal faith in chaps like young Schwiller.

However, it is no longer the role of the big companies to be innovative. It is their function to absorb the trends into mass production. For example Rank Strand, having for some time remained coolly detached from the small boys' moves to update the mini-controls, have quietly absorbed all the innovations and upstaged everyone else with their new Tempus which immediately becomes the definitive mass-market control.

When the ABTT Trade Show started in 1978, it was a homely event with some of the big firms standing aside. Success of the event has now brought them all in to share the action. Let us hope, however, that the ABTT will continue to encourage small firms and especially small non-lighting firms.

This can probably only be achieved by rental discrimination against the biggies – but if these biggies have any sense, they will be happy to encourage the small firms so that they can ultimately absorb the best of them.

One firm that has actually grown from small to large during the three year history of ABTT Trade Shows is TBA (Tim Burnham Associates) and it is interesting (and surely instructive) to note that they have done so by offering service at the top end of the market rather than by offering discounts at the bottom end.

It was good to see old majors like Radcliffe Transport and new minors like Hairaisers on parade. And the stands of Peter Evans Ltd and Packman Research were offering joy to designer and production manager alike.

Spectrum (last year's award winners) are establishing themselves nicely and newcomers Light Works are my tip for the 'firm to watch'.

But if I had any trophy to award personally, it would go without any doubt to Roscolab who continue to be the chaps with the most alert, sympathetic and inventive response to the miscellaneous requirements of our theatre industry.

Their directional diffusers continue to be the best thing to hit lighting design since memory boards. Their colour filters are tops for clarity and now their new prism filters open up new possibilities of diffraction fun. To say nothing of their fog machine, their projection screens, their paints and their scenic materials. Please, don't anyone buy a slash in 1980 without considering Rosco's Slitdrape. And if you cannot think of anything to do with their new LED Tape, then you have no business being in show business.

As long as we have firms like Rosco around, an ABTT Trade Show will be a must!

Photokina (1990)

Way back in the spring, when the leaf gobos were freshly green tinted, I reported on the Parisian start of the great annual fair trading trail across the cities of Europe.

The caravan has just come to rest in Cologne and the circus is preparing to disperse to winter quarters, hopefully to think up some new tricks but more likely just to repackage the old ones. An invite to join in the seminars (without which no trade fair is now complete) gave me an opportunity to check how our industry has fared on its trek through the prime cities of backstage common marketing.

Firstly, I must congratulate the marketing people on their stamina. Despite week after week of endless days demonstrating to people interested in discovering what equipment will not do, and nights entertaining the kind of potential buyers who are lethally boring but justify expense claims, the chaps (and the lamentably few chapesses) are still looking remarkably fit. Only a few individuals looked sufficiently shattered to meet the EEC specification for Knackerwurst.

And their wares? Well, there has been quite a trickle of new stuff since the spring, but with interest rates rising and theatre budgets in free fall, there is definitely caution in the air. The exception is Strand who have invested so heavily in tooling that if the new stuff does not sell, we could well see yet another of the management restructurings upon which their profitability traditionally depends.

Bargain hunters, wishing to pay less for a control desk that does more, will doubtless descend on the new MX series which is full of delights to appeal to knob-happy light persons.

An exhibition stand is no place to assess the quality of light emitted from a spotlight, so we will have to await field reports before discovering whether Quartets offer any serious challenge to Minuettes.

But the real new jewel in the Strand crown is their BC 90 Digital Dimmer. Dimmers do not compete on the glitz appeal of their package. Ideal dimmer racks are those you put in a room, lock the door and lose the key for the next 30 years. With BC 90, the dimmer room key will be required only occasionally and only after the machine has contemplated its digital navel, diagnosed its problem and reported to you in the control room, office, workshop or any pub of your choice.

Digital dimmers are the flavour of the 90s with ADB joining Strand as the big players. In addition to their Eurodim racks for dimmer rooms, they have a very natty range of Eurobloc six-way digital dimmer packs. It is a long time since I lifted a dimmer pack but these seemed infinitely lighter than my memories. Being so lightweight and slender they seem ideal for hanging direct on touring trusses – and we are surely going to see a lot more of this as rigging techniques continue to improve. Photokina opened on the morning after German reunification. But, with one wall down, visitors found that another one was on the Lee stand: the lights were on one side of the fence and the filters on the other.

The new signs, painted on reverse, were ready to swing round as soon as the final details of the management buyout were signed. For filters still call Lee, but if its lights you are after (including Joe Thornley and his Windsor spots) call Lumo.

Photokina is huge. It lasts seven days and I doubt if one could visit every stand in this time. It is mostly about visual images with half the space devoted to the taking and processing of photographs. There is a hi-fi expo in parallel, but its sounds do not intrude.

The absence of the disco and rock industries means a lack of the smoke machines that usually puff and wheeze throughout most exhibitions while manufacturers sing the praises of their environmental friendliness. Photokina is a trade fair for a section of show business which it calls 'Professional Media.'

This is a world of film and television studios to which even the largest opera houses are a poor relation. If you want just one really huge jumbo spotlight that you can just switch on, point at the stage and go to the pub, then this is your supermarket. I jest not. A German flyman assured me that the status of visiting lighting designers is measured by the number of HMI discharge lamps that they can command

Certainly, in all my recent visits to German theatres in the past couple of years, the opening of each and every door has caused the stage to be flooded with a blast of white light of such Star Wars intensity that the actors seek refuge in any morsel of shade.

Photokina was not so much an occasion for discovering new products, but rather more a time for reconfirming the attraction of some of the established goodies like Galaxy and Cantata, newer ones like Talento or trend-setters like the Arri Graphic Tablet. My quality crown goes to Pani, not just for their projectors, but for serving champagne at the correct temperature in properly chilled glasses. I am not being frivolous – people who can get such detail right have an understanding of what getting a show on is all about.

ABTT North Show (1991)

Each backstage trade show has its own individual character. PLASA is where manufacturers have the audacity to charge us an entrance fee to go into their noisy supermarket.

ABTT is where we invite the manufacturers to come to us and display their products in a quieter but more theatrical environment which encourages the constructive user-maker interaction that both sides of our industry need. PLASA has a somewhat cavalier attitude to education: it restricts admission of the very young and charges opera prices for its seminars.

ABTT knows that today's toddlers are tomorrow's technicians and its seminars are freely open to all. But we need both types of show. PLASA for its perspective on the full width of the live entertainment industry: ABTT for its specialised forum for performance areas where financial success tends to be measured in terms of operating surplus rather than simple profit.

I nominate ABTT North as Britain's most user-friendly backstage show. The Opera Theatre and foyer of the Royal Northern College of Music made an ideal venue for this year's event. Spacious, noise-free and smoke-free: an environment to encourage serious discussion between maker and user. A good place to catch up with old chums and make new ones.

It was a comparatively small exhibition, but all the product was relevant to the daily grind of getting ordinary shows on. And the stands were not restricted to light, sound and smoke. Manchester is neither the place nor November the time to attract the product launches of the big boys.

But this gives us a chance to. look at things that have survived. Silhouettes live on. Cantata may now have the performance edge over them, but there remains a healthy future for a spotlight which retains such a tried, trusted and respected basic format that it can easily be upgraded by retrofitting with the latest spare part assemblies.

The Minuette Fresnel is still tops. But how will New Zealand's Selecon fare so far from home? Ask me after Christmas: M and M have sold 25 profiles and ten Fresnels to Richmond where I am lighting Cinders to the Ball. I (and my ponies) hope that my rental budget will run to White Light's VSFX variable speed motors for the snow effects: every time I see these recently introduced units on an exhibition stand, I wonder how we put up for all these years with potter's wheels and their slipping rubber tyres!

However, there were a few brand new products. Keylight of Tameside are proud to point out that their scroller is not only made in Britain but is the only one with a fast cassette loading facility. Prestige Software Systems of Salford used the show to launch themselves into the world of computerised box offices, going for the big market of the small theatres. In addition to holding the plans and printing the tickets, their Box Office Manager runs audit trails, production accounts and a patron database, Software for your own IDM compatible is under 500 quid and you can have a full turnkey system for around £2000.

R and G Services were showing their NOVA range with a common lamphouse that quickly accepts alternative lenses (PC, Fresnel or condenser). Some real common market enterprise here: they import from what was East Germany and sell to the rest of Europe.

The sound chaps spared us their usual demonstrations of high gain. They were professional enough to know that we were serious theatre punters to whom such blasts are irrelevant on an exhibition stand. At a time when sound is, and needs to be, the growth area in theatre technology it was appropriate that the first ABTT Percy Corry Award should be presented to a young sound engineer. The winner was Dale Longworth, the year's most outstanding graduate from Oldham College's BTEC Diploma in Engineering Entertainment. (No, not Entertainment Engineering or Engineering for Entertainment. I checked, knowing how much Percy Corry was fascinated by the niceties of theatre langage.)

Before long there will just have to be some rationalisation in our industry's trade shows. There are now so many that their cost must have a significant effect on the price that manufacturers have to charge us for their goodies. ABTT Trade Shows MUST survive, but perhaps the way forward would be to have alternative years in London and Manchester. Extending the rationalisation to Europe, PLASA could alternate with Cologne's Photokina. If we get the phasing right, London would have an annual show, alternately ABTT and PLASA. Otherwise the product mark-up to pay for exhibitions is going to turn them into shop windows for stuff nobody can afford to buy.

A greener PLASA (1991)

The PLASA exhibition has become more environmentally friendly over the years. There is now noticeably less smoke and only a few isolated pockets where the sound level reaches the threshold of pain. However, the general noise level is certainly something that PLASA will need to improve if it wishes to be considered as important a European lighting showcase as Photokina. At the moment the ambience of the PLASA show falls uncomfortably between the chummy cheap and cheerfulness of ABTT and the serious calm professionalism of Cologne.

But the 1991 PLASA Show did take a considerable step towards green maturity. Some of this is due to the growing presence of manufacturers from the world of what used to be called 'straight theatre'.

Perhaps an even stronger influence is the upmarket aspirations of the younger successful companies widening their product ranges as both they and their original, now loyal, customers gradually become absorbed into the establishment.

But the major influence on this show was economic recession. And, by and large, it was a good influence. Because hardly anyone can afford them we had much less visual pollution from mindlessly gyrating lights dancing to random programmes.

We were spared yet another batch of control systems which do things because a computer can do them rather than because they are needed to light a show. Indeed it is many years since we have seen such wise spending of research and development budgets – spending to benefit both them and us. Strand presented a basketful of cost-effective mods to many of their long runners: nothing sensational, just sensible little upgrades to make the stuff more efficient and user-friendly.

Strand's most effective recession beating strategy has been to get Andy Collier back in the engine room where he has revitalised the content and graphics of their literature. He is also the man behind the re-emergence of Strand's commitment to education which has been firmly on their back burner in recent years.

Teatro has faced up to its customer's recession-hit budgets by getting back to basics. After all, what is a spotlight but a lamp, a lens and a reflector in a box! Everybody uses the same lamps and most use the same lenses. The Lito box may be basic but it has Italian styling and the range is so cheap that Teatro were the only people prepared to display a price tag. These Lito spots are additional to the main Teatro range which goes from strength to strength with its distinctive red bands becoming an increasingly familiar sight to theatregoers.

Red bands are about to become even more familiar because they are part of the image of the luminaire debut of Zero 88 who have diversified from their control base and are all set to challenge the world of Minuettes and Preludes. For those whose hobby is spot spotting, the key difference is that Teatro have the red band at the top while Zero 88 have it at the bottom.

The recession caused CCT some discomfort earlier this year but Messrs Hindle, Manners and Watling were on a stand festooned with silhouettes to assure us that it was business as usual. Luff have been rescued: too late for a stand at the show but those old Strand stalwart refugees, John Ball and Richard Harris, after an excursion into sound mixing, were handing out cards to prove that they are back in the lighting business.

The Pani BP4 projector has long been the international standard HMI for scene projection, with the BP6 Gold for those who need even more brightness. Now comes the BP 12 platinum which is too bright for the stages of even the biggest opera houses but just right for outdoor mega block-busters. The problems of projection in limited depth are going to be eased considerably with Pani's new superwide 11cm objective lens. Slide changers have been further refined and the fade from the new grey-scale mechanical dimmer is impeccable. But Pani serves a market which is relatively immune to such minor hiccups as economic recessions!

A welcome for the European debut of Selecon whose New Zealand profiles have colonised Sydney Opera House and who have improved Fresnels by the simple expedient of going back to a bigger diameter lens while contriving to keep the body small.

Good also, to find Howard Eaton at the show. Howard's product range is not based on some deeply profound marketing strategy. It is just a collection of stuff that people needed for particular shows and Howard, as a practical man of the theatre, found a way to make. Once made as specials, these items were discovered to have a wider appeal. Howard Eaton and Pani were probably the only truly consumer led firms in the whole show.

Who gets the medal for looking ahead? Is it Zero 88 for anticipating that a pair of I.5kW parcans will stimulate demand for 15amp dimmers? Or is it Pani for knowing that the really upmarket scroller will be the one which scrolls three dichroics within a single unit for subtractive mixing? Or does it go to those who share my concern that the MIDI might possibly be the greatest threat since the clicktrack to keeping live entertainment live?

My product of the year does exist. Although it missed its flight from the Rosco factory, Michael Hall has given me Stan Miller's word that quarter Hamburg will be here in time for the pantomime season. Meanwhile Rosco have joined the club of those who aspire to topple Rainbow from the scroller throne with a model that talks all the standard analogue and digital protocols, accepting varying scroll lengths from three to 24 frames: a noble gesture allowing the user to save on filter costs. Their confidence is backed by a five year (parts and labour) guarantee.

By the next PLASA we shall be well into the threats and promises of the much heralded European 1992. How will it affect our industry? Free trade is not only about dropping national barriers: we will be able to buy CCT silhouettes from any Strand dealer. Will manufacturers move more towards selling direct or through retailers? Either way, both Strand and ADB are increasingly looking the wrong size for Europe. If their masters, Rank and Siemens, wanted to strike a buy and sell deal, would the EEC equivalent of our monopolies commission intervene?

Melbourne Conference 1991

Australia, like most of the world, is in recession. But, headlining their story The Bonanza of The Phantom Economy and A Phantom led Recovery, Melbourne's Sunday Age declared: 'If ever there was an antidote for Victoria's recessed and depressed economy The Phantom of the Opera seems to be it.'

The local Tourist Authority calculates that Phantom has generated more than 100 million Australian dollars (about £46 million) in six months. This includes the audience's accommodation, meals, taxis and tickets but not their airfares which must be considerable with 40,000 people from New Zealand alone.

So Melbourne's World Congress Centre was an appropriate venue for Pro Light and Sound Show Expo 91, billed as Australia's biggest ever professional light and sound show. Be heard, Be seen, Be there screamed the publicity. So I went. Well, who would refuse a ticket to Oz to join Richard Pilbrow and BBC TV Sound's Larry Goodson as the overseas voices in the seminars.

Getting us to go was probably the easiest part of the job for the maestro who made it all happen – ex-pat pom Paul Chapell who is currently technical supremo of the Adelaide Festival Centre. It was he who got the technokit makers and their distributors to set up stall in the exhibition (only one major declined but has acknowledged the mistake and booked space for next time). It was Paul who persuaded the punters to fly the vast distances that are involved in even the shortest interstate journey. And a large contingent of Kiwis crossed the Tasmanian sea.

All the usual international product manufacturers were represented plus several locals including Selecon and Bytecraft, the expanding twins whose rapidly growing internationalism is poised to make an impact in the UK. New Zealand's Selecon, run by a bunch of real theatre elex, has an interesting range which includes the 1.2kW profile chosen for the re-equipping of Sydney Opera House.

Australia's Bytecraft are into all manner of digital innovations from dimmers to the controls for the Victorian State Theatre's new flying system with hydraulics designed in-house. Bytecraft gave me the most confident response I have yet had to my recurring query about when do we get 24 Volt 500 Watt electronic transformers to put in spotlights operating in a hostile environment and without fans.

But none of the manufacturers produced any new gear to make me shout eureka! So in the seminars I offered my view that the product of the year will be Rosco 161. With Rosco having overcome the quality control problems of making a quarter Hamburg diffuser (it is so very close to being clear), I proposed that the traditional defocussing of profile spots to get soft edges is finally dead. Hamburg and half-Hamburg frosts have made the practice almost obsolescent: quarter Hamburg makes it virtually obsolete. I also declared Fesnels dead. We will have to carry on using the old Fresnels (there are so many about), but it is surely folly to buy new ones when there is now such a wide range of diffusers to progressively soften a focus spot with a PC lens.

The seminars were well attended despite being very expensive. But they qualified under Australian Government rules for mandatory spending by theatres on in-service training. Discussions were good and positive. After all this is the land where such genteel English as get-outs become bump-outs; although, come to think of it, a bump-out seems more restrained than a Scottish chuck-out!

New technologies were to the fore, particularly remotely focused lights and Autocad. And some lively forums included 'Are Consultants Fees Really Necessary?'

All the guest speakers gave personal view talks and, to my shame, I missed Nigel Levings who, Richard Pilbrow tells me, was brilliant. My absence was due to sleeping off the fruits of the vineyard.

Did I really sit with a couple of hundred technicians in a Melbourne tapas bar watching flamenco and discussing such subjects as Robert Nesbitt, light conosle foot pushes and how to rig a wiffenpooff? Mostly with Keith Yates whose London Palladium expertise has been fundamental to Sydney Opera House since it opened. But these informal sessions are what theatre expos are all about. Pro Lighting and Sound Expo 92 is fixed for May 14 through 16 in Sydney, with Brisbane pencilled for 93.

Rimini Magis Seminar

The primary purpose of any trade fair is to catalyse interaction between user and supplier. But it can also provide a forum for cross-fertilisation between an industry's various sections which tend to operate in parallel but with a considerable degree of isolation. Our entertainment lighting industry is at a point in its development when there is a generally recognised need for more cross-fertilisation between the procedures and technologies of the various live and mechanical performance media. The equipment on the stands stimulates a great deal of informal contact: we all roam the exhibitions looking for ideas, following up interesting observations by picking the brains of the sales engineers. But there is a growing urgency for the various lighting users to sit down a little bit more formally to talk with each other and with suppliers to establish where needs integrate and where they diverge. When this happens, we usually find that our needs are closer than we thought!

Magis chose the new light sources as a subject for just such an afternoon. Three lamp manufacturers (Osram, Philips and Sylvania) presented their view of the technology, and a quartet of lighting designers talked about their specialist areas as light source users. Pino Pinori (cinema) and Aldo Solbiati (television) discussed lighting for their respective camera while I dealt with the theatre's human eye. Renato Neri covered the needs of 'live shows', the mega star concerti where the lighting has to bridge the needs of both the human eye and the video camera.

A major theme to emerge from the manufacturers was their apparent polarisation (I hesitate to call it war) on the respective merits of the established HMI and the newer MSR (Medium Source Rare Earth) lamps. The symposium listened but seemed reluctant to discuss the issue: I suspect that most of those present are waiting, like me, for hands-on experience with MSR lamps in appropriate luminaires under show conditions. However Mr Van Den Plas of Philips put a case that whetted this particular user's appetite for MSR.

Although there was some mention of the differing quality of light from various types of sources, much of the discussion was concerned with the potential of the high intensity available from discharge lamps generally.

Users of a film or video eye are naturally much concerned with matters of colour temperature, while live show people home in on the dimming problem. Few users seek an increase in overall intensity levels. Film and camera sensitivity do not require it and the iris in the human eye closes up in response to more brightness. Lighting is all about balance. In the 1960s the great American designer Howard Bay said: "all theatres should have one 5kW light but only one … give them two and the dramatic effect will cancel out." A bit extreme perhaps, but nevertheless fundamentally true.

While a major attraction for lighting designers is the ability to make positive incisive lighting statements which cut through general tungsten halogen stage light levels, the really big advantages (and consequently potential market) are in large venues with long throws. With venues increasing in audience capacity as a response to economic pressures, it can be a very long distance from spotlight to stage. Only the light from discharge lamps is sufficiently intense to make the journey. Discharge lamps have long been the norm for follow spotting but are likely to find increasing general use, both in fixed and remotely movable instruments.

While the partial electrical dimming achievable with discharge sources can be acceptable in the studio, full control down to blackout is demanded on the stage. This means mechanical dimming and is mainly a financial rather than a technical problem. Remote mechanical dimming has been in regular use for more than a decade. Pani use motorised glasses, graded from clear through to opaque, on their scenic projectors while they and others have also used remotely operated Venetian blinds. Diaphragms are another valuable technique, probably at their most currently sophisticated state of mechanical dimming no longer seems the hazard (or indeed the unacceptable expense) that it seemed when we got our first CSI lamps 20 years ago. And if we are going to go to the expense of putting remote facilities on a spotlight, we might as well do it on a bright one!

Colour temperature has never had the importance in theatre that it has in film and video. Stage lighting designers have become used to taking into account the reddening consequences of dimming when choosing colour filters. However, mechanical dimming offers the bonus of maintaining colour temperature throughout a fade.

But my own problems in using discharge lamp followspots (since the first 400 Watt CSI in 1967) have not arisen from their quoted colour temperatures but from mismatching of pairs. This has quite often been initial mismatching between new lamps, but more usually a lack of balance developing due to differential rates of colour shift. The colour shift curves presented in support of MSR sources are encouraging and I look forward to checking them with my eyes (in a theatre, of course, not in a lab.).

A cheering note for theatre's cost accountants (if any there be): with discharge sources, quoted lamp life has some practical significance in predicting how long a lamp will last, whereas under electrical dimming life is virtually incalculable.

The manager in me welcomes the cost-effective design improvements underway in halogen lamps, but my lighting designer's eyes tell me that halogen stage lighting has been very close to the end of the line for some time now. Future development is likely to mean only minor refinements in optics and mechanics plus a lot of badge engineering. Halogen spots will continue to be the backbone of theatre lighting rigs, but any improvements are more likely to be noticeable in the budgets than on the stages.

I remain hungry for low-voltage sources. Apart from the bulk and weight of their integral transformers, my 1961 Reiche & Vogel beamlights (24 Volt 500 Watt) were just about the finest tool that I ever had at my disposal. We still await heat stable electronic transformers. But at Rimini, Osram penetrated the usual gloom and doom on this topic with some hope for the day after tomorrow.

Meanwhile, my attention at exhibitions will concentrate on digital remote mechanical dimmers; and for static spotlights even more than for moving ones. Because, despite all the undoubted joys of being able to remote all the functions of a moving light, the most critical feature of a light beam is the angle at which it strikes the actor or object. Shifting this angle means physically repositioning the whole light. Or using a lot of lights. So the approach is still normally going to mean a rig incorporating a lot of fixed instruments, even when some remotely movable lights are included to speed refocusing and offer opportunities for dynamic effects.

Lamps are the fundamental source of our light, and the history of the development of entertainment lighting shows virtual total dependence on the pace of lamp research development and manufacture. The dialogue has traditionally been between spotlight manufacturer and the lamp giants. To include the user is rare, and Magis deserves our thanks for stimulating a dialogue that should surely continue.

NZATT Third international conference (1993)

New Zealand has a similar geographical area to the British Isles but the population is less than our unemployed. Nevertheless this low population density is matched with so much live theatre activity that the Kiwis rate high in any international headcount of theatregoers as a proportion of population.

New Zealand's backstagers formed NZATT ten years ago, using aspects of ABTT and USITT as a model. Although the original NZATT acronym has been retained, 'theatre technician' as a description of those of us who support the actor tends to lack weight in a world populated by chiefs of this and generals of that, with every infant ambition targeted on job titles such as Chief General Executive Director of Consultative Support, at the very least. So New Zealand's Association of Theatre Technicians has become an Association for Theatre Craft, Design and Technology.

NZATT is thriving very successfully indeed. But, if I am going to make statements like that, I have to declare my interest and reveal that not only am I an honorary life member but I am the proud possessor of an NZATT Hook Clamp – plated not with chromium, or even silver, but gold.

NZATT held their third International Conference at the Aotea Centre in Auckland over the last weekend of May, and a large attendance indicated that only the very minimum crews had stayed at home to run the scheduled performances. Friday afternoon was devoted to a walking tour of Auckland City venues, Saturday evening hosted a revolving dinner atop the Telecom Tower and Sunday afternoon offered Carmen.

This left three half days for intensive technical sessions organised as 15 slots in three parallel specialised streams focusing on Craft, Design and Technology. Coffee breaks were held in the Trade Show exhibition area and the Aotea's studio theatre hosted half-hourly moving light shows.

Prominent at the trade show were New Zealand's 'big two' manufacturers: Theatrelight and Selecon, specialising in controls and spotlights respectively. Their home grown products form the backbone of New Zealand theatre lighting installations, although Selecon has made the strongest impact on the international scene. Hardly surprising when the world is awash with control makers, whereas spotlight manufacturing is concentrated in a small number of firms.

Although still relatively small, Selecon has been able to join the big league by applying the sort of lateral thinking that makes their latest PC Spot the current world leader in beam quality. So much so that they will doubtless be paid the ultimate honour of being cloned by the big boys before the year is out.

Most of the familiar international product was on display: the world and his wife all seem to have New Zealand agents, although there are some unfamiliar bedfellows.

A couple of years ago Auckland opened a new opera house called the Aotea Centre. Backstage is a good well-equipped touring house but it is difficult to find any kind words for the auditorium other than to applaud the comfort of the seats and plushiness of the carpets. Otherwise it is a vast concrete barn, institutionally painted in browns and creams.

I never imagined that it was possible to build a theatre so large, yet holding only 2000 audience: I have rarely felt so isolated in a full house as when attending the current Carmen.

In a conference session which started with discussion around the set model and then moved to examining the set's realisation on stage, the designer and production manager/lighting designer took us through the design process, including the moment when the opera company's directorate made a rather late marketing decision that the location should revert from the proposed anonymous motorway to recognisable Seville.

Despite a leaden acoustic which inhibits any hint of romantic opulence from the pit, this was a good performance with Adria Firestone as one of the best Carmens I have heard or seen – there was no doubt at all about where this Carmen would roll her cigars!

The sadness of the Aotca Centre is that its shortcomings were predicted by the local theatre and architectural communities. It is early sixties erected in the late 80s.

It even fails to exploit a lavish city centre site. Something positive will eventually have to be done about the acoustic, although an essential beginning has already been made by a conductor who stopped a concert and despatched the orchestra leader to switch off the computerised microphones of the assisted resonance system.

I have a hunch that the acoustic problem is partly, but only partly, psychological. In a curious way, I suspect that the sound would be better if the decorative scheme were more luscious.

It is perhaps ironical that the foyer just happens to make a splendid concert hall with a lively close sound. We live in an age when conversions are often more successful than purpose-built theatres, and Auckland is no exception. The old Custom House provides a sympathetic space for an innovative company and the Old Pump House needs no further accolade than to say that it miniaturises Snape Maltings but retains its own identity.

My view that NZATT is thriving is based on several factors additional to the lively debate at its conference. In particular, the AGM revealed a healthy level of activity in the regional branches, an extensive programme of short courses and an expanding magazine. Plus some forward looking outreach in the shape of a lighting design award scheme for schools, with NZATT members going to see, assess, and comment upon the lighting of school productions.

Would any sponsor care to charter a 747 for a weekend so that the ABTT membership could seek inspiration in New Zealand?

Showtech Berlin (1993)

Showtech is unique. This is the exhibition where you have to go searching for the lighting equipment. Yes, the lighting manufacturers are really in a minority.

They are all there (anyone wishing to be considered in the serious lighting league has no option) but they are swamped by all the other aspects of theatre technology. There is not much sound gear and it is switched off. There is no smoke. The avenues are wide and it all takes place in air-conditioned daylight. This is Europe's premier environmentally friendly backstage show.

Lights were even outnumbered by chairs and, if the best of these represents the trend in European seating, even those as wide-bodied as me can anticipate a more comfortable future in the theatre. Unless, of course, Britain fails to ratify the European Treaty.

Lots of ticketing systems to computerise your box office: a big market since a lot of German theatres still use the traditional card, small but boldly printed and fitting much more neatly into the wallet than many of the newer under-inked computer-generated flimsies. Costumiers, drapers and prop-makers in abundance. Hardware on every scale from basic ironmongery to the engineering complexities of the operatic stage.

Like antique fairs, theatre shows always have a considerable amount of inter-stand activity. Showtech seemed particularly active in this respect with dealerships being traded both inside the EEC and between east and west. Recently privatised firms from the east were seeking a market share. One product range that particularly caught the eye was some neat simple mechanical shutters for discharge lamps, including a low pressure sodium batten unit available through Britain's R&G Group whose Nova spotlight range originated behind the old wall.

For the statistically minded, the technology displayed by 185 exhibitors from 14 countries was inspected by 4,450 backstagers from 21 countries. Despite the recession, large venues are being planned or are already under construction in Europe. And despite arts subsidy cuts triggered by reunification costs, Germany is still a big market.

Cuts are relative and German cut budgets are still big, even huge, by our standards. Moreover, cost-cutting is not being allowed to interfere with the essential refurbishing of stage installations completed during the massive building boom of 1945-65 and now failing to meet current technical or safety standards. In response to cuts, re-equipping with new technology is being seen as an opportunity for rationalisation to achieve the same performance levels with a reduced workforce, or boost these levels without increasing the number of employees.

Operational efficiency was the lead topic discussed by the 350 participants in the Showtech seminars arranged by DTHG, the German equivalent of ABTT. One major theme, and the reason for my invited presence, was a debate on the potential operational benefits, artistically and economically, of including a lighting designer as a member of the production team. Germany, with a few Central European countries operating in a similar tradition of high subsidy and daily rep change, is the only remaining part of the world without lighting designers.

There is a lot of excellent lighting to be seen, although the tendency is to rely on a sequence of isolated momentary images of memorable dramatic impact. It is what happens, or rather does not happen, between these lovely frozen moments that demonstrates the lack of, and need for, someone to take lighting design responsibility. Increased artistic aspirations for the use of light, coupled with new technological possibilities, have become too complex for director and designer to rely on inspirational programming of the technicians at extended lighting rehearsals.

Somebody needs to get down to hard graft specialist planning at the drawing board or CAD screen.

But it is not art that will bring lighting designers into general use in the German theatre. Like everywhere else, the initial motivation will be the commercial advantages of minimising expensive stage time with a lot of crew waiting around. Economic change has now made the lighting designer inevitable in Germany. The main resistance appears to stem from the technical directors who are naturally concerned about the twice daily repertoire changeovers. But the Showtech Exhibition had the answers: robotic lights and rock rigging.

The main social event was a mass visit to the new Jazzlegs revue at the Friedrichstadtpalast with its 2000 seats and a stage so vast that even a chorus line of 60 makes a negligible impact on an audience whose involvement is defeated by the scale. The interval foyer trapeze artists were much more fun. This is a theatre which needs designs from a John Napier and inspiration from a Cameron Mackintosh who might even be able to entice Harry Kupfer, director of the brilliant new production of Handel's Guilio Cesare the Komische Oper. We could then look forward to an exciting Friedrichspalast at the next Berlin Showtech which is scheduled for May 30 to June 1 in 1995.

Showlight Bradford (1993)

If all the theatre technology trade shows in the world were placed end to to end, they would more than fill the calendar

Manning the stands is a major proportion of the job description of the industry's sales and marketing executives. However, the salary costs of this are probably cancelled out by the savings gained from having the research and development chaps sniff around competitors stands rather than invest in expensive laboratories. Few of us punters who go to the shows have any dosh for serious buying. We are there to meet our friends: the hardware on the stands provides useful conversation pieces and, who knows, we might occasionally find something new and interesting.

But every four years there is an exception. It is called Showlight.

Previous appearances were in London, New York and Amsterdam. Number four has just been held in Bradford. Showlight is a product of the CIE (Commission lntenationale Eclairage). Very few of those of us who labour in the lighting industry know what this body is or what it does other than that it invented the international luminaire symbols a long time ago. Even fewer of us have even felt any need to discover anything further. I was once a member of a CIE committee and I was never quite sure who we were or why. But the importance of committees lies not in their constitution but in their membership and, above all, in their leader.

For as long as anyone can remember the showbiz lighting committee of the CIE has been chaired by Ken Ackerman, now retired but formerly the studio equipment planning supremo at the BBC during the critical growth years of television technology. Ackerman and his committee are the Showlight catalysts and after attending three out of four, I am confidently prepared to declare Showlight as lighting conference number one.

There are a number of reasons for Showlight's success. Perhaps the key one is that the equipment exhibition is an appendage to the conference sessions, not the other way around. Indeed the exhibition closes when the conference (or colloquium as they prefer to call it) is in session. All the makers and marketeers go to the lecture room to listen to the papers and contribute to the discussions. As a result there is a real interaction between makers and users rather than the lip service which is so often paid elsewhere.

Anyone delivering a paper has to get to the point: with the exception of four distinguished guests who are allowed half-an-hour, all speakers get the red light towards the end of their allocated 15 minutes.

However, all delegates do get a good chance to visit the exhibition: it is held in the hall where everyone adjourns for the hour long coffee breaks and even longer lunches. All stands are the same small size with just enough room for a few small pieces of equipment, a couple of chairs and a pile of literature. The scale is human: Showlight is about how to use technology rather than just rejoice in it for its own sake. And there really is interaction between stage and studio: Showlight is about film, theatre and television lightpersons talking and listening to each other.

The Bradford event centred on the National Museum of Film, Photography and Television, with the exhibition located in the Alhambra Studio. Visits were made to the Alhambra, West Yorkshire Playhouse and Emmerdale Farm Studios. With a space film at the Imax Cinema, a civic reception and a trip on Rocket in steam at York Railway Museum followed by dinner on the platform between the restored Royal trains, serenaded by British Rail Intercity Silver Band, there was little time for such mundane activities as going to bed.

The highlight was undoubtedly the talk by doyen lighting cameraman Freddie Young illustrated by clips of his 75 years of film making from *Goodbye Mr Chips* to *Lawrence of Arabia* and *Dr Zhivago*. Richard Pilbrow, briefly back home to celebrate the arrival of his first grandchild, took a look at the future with particular focus on robotics and their control.

John (Spitting Image) Henshall tried, with considerable success, to convince us that digital imaging would replace film emulsion, while Patrick Woodroffe speculated in a general way about the future of lighting designers of megastar live concerts.

Most papers either considered the past, summarised the present or speculated in a general way about the future. But Asbjorn Hagen, bead of lighting for Norwegian Television put himself on the line by declaring his plans for lighting the 1994 Winter Olympics – now we know what to watch out for. Much of Showlight revolved around robotic lights and their control. With remote pan, tilt and focus now well established, research is shifting towards finding the best ways of moving instruments along a truss.

There was, of course, a lot of computer talk. Indeed some were heard to mutter that there was a little bit too much. Perhaps this was because papers tended to concentrate on control, data-tracking and document drawing; whereas the real excitements now emerging, particularly in America, are in computer visualisation.

These techniques allow accurate simulation of how a scene will look under various lighting conditions to be computer generated and manipulated on a video screen. Production meetings centred on pictures rather than words are becoming a possibility. Their reality could well form the lead theme for Showlight 97.

Pro Audio and Light Asia '96 in Singapore – Obedient Lights

Automated luminaires with computerised remote control of all their functions are often called intelligent lights. The lighting possibilities of these sophisticated sources are virtually unlimited and they can be relied upon for total accuracy in repeating all movements which have been recorded. But we, the users, have to decide what effects will enhance the show and then programme the lights to achieve those effects. So I prefer to think of them as obedient lights. To anyone wondering how to maximise the effects of these dynamic lights, I offer a few thoughts.

Every show has to be paced: lighting is like music in that it loses impact if every number has the same tempo and rhythm. Light movement is an integral feature of today's popular music and is a firm part of audience expectation. But the contribution of light movements to the picture and their timing need to relate to the structure of the music because any impression that they are random will reduce the impact of both sound and vision.

Is the music in two or three beats (or multiples) to the bar? Most pop and rock rhythm is based on a two-beat rather than three-beat configuration. However, getting the lights to fit the music is dependent on the way which a choreographer shapes the movement of the performers. Listening to the choreographers' counting during rehearsal can help. How many beats are they counting for each self-contained fragment of dance? It is surprising how often choreographers work on an eight-beat count. So an eight-beat chase sequence is frequently the pattern which is most likely to offer a comfortable fit to the music.

The time dimension is not only caused by the movements of the light but also by the movements of performers and cameras in relation to the light. So we need to prepare a palette of lighting effects which can be used solo or combined in a series of permutations which can be integrated with the cameras. A point to take note with actively moving lights is that there may be less need to cut between cameras. It would be more effective to hold cameras still on an extended zoom or track.

Effects have to be unveiled gradually. Never reveal all the possibilities in the first number. Variety shows have to build up through a series of ever increasing climaxes, interspersed with quieter moments, to culminate in a knock-out grand finale. This is when the light is visible. But they can also be changed when the light intensity is at zero. This is an effective alternative to live dynamic movements, especially when a series of luminaires, programmed to move when they are temporarily blacked out, are used in a chasing sequence.

There are several ways of enhancing dramatic moments: a simultaneous left/right pan and up/down tilt so that the light can sweep in any required curving arc, zoom the focus to produce various sized beams from a tight pin spot to spreading flood, project gobo images using sweep, zoom and focus or have a virtually infinite change of colours.

There are also other subtle possibilities like slowly changing colour sequences, independently focused onto the setting or costumes or the atmospheric backlight, subtle texture changes using out-of-focus break-up gobos. In some cases, the lighting can slowly become tighter and tighter towards the end of a sad or romantic number, with a silhouette on the last note. Then, after a momentary pause flash on a complete contrast in colour, intensity and movement to break the tension and to generate applause.

At the end of the day, the biggest temptation is to do something just because it can be done. So the rule is that an effect should only be used if the show calls for it. With singers, I like to see the natural facial skin tones maintained throughout so that no matter how crazy the the effects are, the audience can still read the eyes of the performers and their emotions.

STR Georgian Theatre conference in Richmond (Yorks) (2008)

When the Society for Theatre Research was inaugurated in 1948, Richmond's Georgian Theatre had been rediscovered but not yet restored. So it was appropriate that the Society should hold its diamond jubilee conference in this Yorkshire gem of a 1788 auditorium that was restored in 1963 and refurbished in 2003 – on both occasions with the benefit of the scholarly expertise of STR members.

In such a setting, the conference theme just had to be the Georgian Playhouse, and the wide ranging discussions on the theatre activity of the century from 1750 to 1850 were enhanced by being held on a stage and in an auditorium which housed the rise and fall of one of the greatest

Georgian Theatre in Richmond (Yorks)

periods in our dramatic heritage. Two dozen papers reported ongoing research to uncover details of every aspect of performance and there was something for everyone, no matter how specialised their interest.

As a backstager, my particular highlights included an Iain Mackintosh explanation, precise and concise, of architectural geometry based on a rod measuring sixteen feet and six inches. Then there was Pieter van der Merwe on Clarkson Stanfield's scenery for Macready's 1842 revival of Acis and Galatea followed by Pavel Slavko and Peter Perina from Cesky Krumlov demonstrating the quality of light generated by different candle recipes and manufacturing techniques.

However, theatres are for performing drama rather than just talking about it and so, as the centrepiece of the weekend, Richmond mounted, for three nights only but most certainly worthy of an extended afterlife, an entertainment directed and led by Timothy West. After barely half the rehearsal time of weekly rep, we were treated to a polished evening of bravura ensemble from a starry company including Jenny Agutter and Charles Kay. Scenes, songs, and anecdotes about 18th century actors and audiences celebrated the period when Samuel Butler built and ran the Richmond Theatre as part of the Yorkshire circuit. This was followed by an example of the afterpiece without which no evening in a Georgian theatre was complete. The choice of David Garrick's Lethe was particularly appropriate as he wrote it to satirise the fashions and foibles of the society of his day. Remove their wigs and, no surprise, these characters are easily recognisable as today's poseurs.

Faced with this acting tour de force, it may seem churlish to complain that the forestage was lowered to provide an orchestra pit for the harpsichord. With action confined within the proscenium plus only a small apron, we were denied the full Georgian experience of action thrust into the auditorium. The proffered reason was that the woodland set, Britain's oldest remaining scenery, dated from 1836 when forestages were being cut back. Logical perhaps but surely an occasion when the reasoning of scholars should have given way to the instinct of artists.

The forestage issue also arose in a fascinating presentation by the Colonial Williamsburg Foundation on their research and design towards a reconstruction of the Georgian theatre architecture erected in colonial Virginia. The need for the assistance of archaeologists to determine the original footprint of the theatre emphasises that this is a reconstruction rather than a restoration project. A virtual reality tour through the design revealed a feature that is missing from most European restorations – an orchestra pit in front of the forestage. In both Richmond and Bury St Edmunds we have a choice of forestage or orchestra pit – either but not both. Music was an intrinsic part of Georgian theatre production and it would be wonderful to hear it in its proper architectural context – even if the consequent loss of seating capacity made it just an occasional treat.

Pivotal to the conference, and indeed to the STR Jubilee, was the co-publication with the British Library of a magnificent facsimile of James Winston's The Theatric Tourist of 1805. Many of the 24 plates of provincial theatres, none closer to London than Edmonton, are familiar from books and exhibitions but never before easily available in the context of Winston's text. This is an exciting book to which I shall be returning in these backstage pages.

Winston's career included management of Drury Lane and co-founding the Garrick Club of which he was first secretary. His vast accumulation of material on a further 250 Georgian theatres is spread across the world's libraries and David Wilmore is researching the notebooks, sketches and watercolours. Meanwhile James Fowler gave us a tantalising glimpse of the V&A holdings.

A Georgian theatre may have segregated its audience into pit, boxes and gallery but the intimacy of its auditorium united all sections of society in a common response to the drama on its stage. In her keynote address, Jane Moody suggested that this played a positive role in identifying national identity – even helping to define, for the 18th century, the elusive Britishness that our politicians currently seek to identify.

SIBMAS Glasgow (2008)

ALD members may be familiar with such acronyms as ABTT, PLASA, SBTD, SMA, STLD and USITT, but how about SIBMAS? It is the Société Internationale des Bibliothèques et des Musées des Arts du Spectacle – or, being one of these organisations where every word, whether spoken or written, is mandatory bilingual – The International Association of Libraries and Museums of the Performing Arts.

SIBMAS members are pivotal in ensuring that lighting design is accorded its proper importance in the archiving of productions for posterity and so, with curators and librarians expressing a growing awareness of this, I was invited to give a keynote address on *How did the lighting look?* – *interpreting the evidence* at this summer's biennial SIBMAS Conference in Glasgow.

In 40 minutes and 60 images (photos, drawings, plans, plots, magic sheets, etc., etc.) I tried to explain the extent of the lighting impression that can be deduced from still and moving production images, designs and documentation. Beginning with oil and candles, I discussed how the evidence has changed as lighting has developed, particularly with digital imaging and with CAD processes that generate their own archive in an easily stored format. In the spirit of the Focus motto – more art, less tools – I assured them that the easy part to decipher was the equipment, suggesting that understanding the contribution of lighting to an archived production involved three part analysis

- What light did the audience see – consciously and subconsciously?
- What dramaturgy motivated this use of light?
- How was this use of light achieved?

The response was encouraging. Delegates from several theatre museums across Europe took me aside to confide that they realised it was time to review their policy for acquiring and preserving lighting material. There were invitations to visit and I have already accepted one to Paris to see some of the lighting treasures in the Bibliothèque Nationale. From Ohio has come DOCUMENTING: Lighting Design (ISBN 978-0-932610-20-1) recently published by the American Theatre Library Association as Volume 25 of their Performing Arts Resources Series.

This book includes summaries of the scope of the lighting material deposited in the Library of Congress, New York Public Library, The Shubert Archive, Wisconsin Historical Society, and the university collections at Harvard, Ohio State, Pennsylvania State and Yale. The bibliography of lighting literature is concise but comprehensive, and there are supportive chapters on lighting's history and its technology. Libraries are a key teaching resource and so there are stimulating discussions on the history of stage lighting education and on the role of archival research in teaching lighting design. It is a book which I am sure will help to raise the profile of lighting archives – and consequently be a factor in raising the status of the lighting designer's contribution to the art of performance.

Throughout my talk to SIBMAS I emphasised how it is the juxtaposition of images, designs and documents that triggers clues to the contribution that light made to an archived production. However, I concluded with this warning about the dangers of subjecting lighting archives to an excess of rigorous academic analysis.

The most important material for capturing that elusive essence of how did the lighting look? will always be images. But an experienced eye researching the documentation can uncover considerable information about the light design process, its dramaturgy, and the methodology of its realisation.

However, while explanations of whys and wherefores can be fascinating and indeed useful, I would caution against giving too much weight to them. Although lighting designers rely on scientific logic to translate visual ideas into reality, lighting design – like all art – owes little to logic. It is based on illogical decisions made from a gut feeling that is derived from the absorption of tangible information tempered with intangible instincts. Asked to explain my work: "Why did you do that?", quite often the only answer I have been able to offer has been "Why not?"

Like the other members of the scenography team, lighting designers tend, by inclination and education, to be visual thinkers. Although we have to attempt to 'verbalise the visual' in order to communicate within the creative team, for much of what we do with light there is no further justification than "if it looks right – and all the creative team, not just the lighting designer, agrees that it looks right – then it is right".

So, although we can capture some of the essence of how the lighting looked, the search for why it looked that way can perhaps be rather more elusive. The subtleties remain the privilege of those who were at the performance. And what they saw – or thought they saw – is unique to each member of the audience's vision and perception. In that key respect the lighting is no different from all the other intangibles that make each performance unique.

6 BOOK REVIEWS

Winston: The Theatric Tourist
– facsimile edition

In the early 1960s I splashed out my three guinea fee for an article in The Stage on acquiring a print of the Georgian Theatre in Lewes. I knew nothing of James L. Winston or The Theatric Tourist, his monthly partwork commenced in 1804 as a genuine collection of correct views with brief and authentic accounts of all the provincial theatres in the United Kingdom.

My ignorance remained until the 1975 Georgian Playhouse exhibition at the Hayward where I found my Lewes print among the full set of 24 displayed from Winston's book. Falling in love with the word theatric, I borrowed Winston's title to record my own travels in a long running series in Cue magazine and a subsequent book. During the brief period of enlightenment when we had a Theatre Museum, I drooled over the Winston prints on every visit.

But Winston's words? I never got around to organising myself into seeing one of the scarce copies scattered across the world's libraries. However, in celebration of their sixtieth anniversary, The Society for Theatre Research, in association with the British Library, have now produced a truly magnificent facsimile edition.

Winston planned 90 theatres but the project stopped after 24 and in 1805 all 24 were issued in a bound volume that forms the basis of this facsimile edited by Iain Mackintosh with an erudite introduction by Marcus Risden, librarian at the Garrick Club. Since Winston was a co-founder of the Garrick, serving as its first secretary and librarian, Risdell's input is neatly appropriate.

All the plates (approximately A4 in size) are exteriors, executed with such skill that one wishes with considerable fervour that he had included some interiors. Winston's interests did extend to all parts of the playhouse and at Plymouth in 1803 the whole of the interior was rebuilt under the immediate and sole direction of, and from a drawing made by Mr Winston, as complete as any out of London. But this was an

Winston's Lewes Theatre

era when the architect provided a shell for fitting out by other specialist hands – the carpenters and scenic artists – and in The Theatric Tourist Winston is primarily concerned with the architecture. His text offers tantalising glimpses of fitting out but it was an era in which the inside of a theatre had a clearly established norm whereas the exterior came in many variations.

Of Richmond (Surrey, not Yorkshire) Winston declares that internally considered, we may pronounce this house a model for theatre architects. Before the curtain are commodious boxes, and a roomy pit, with every convenience. Behind it are twenty-four feet depth of stage, terminated by an arch beyond which the stage may occasionally be lengthened twenty feet. Such a general description could be a puff written for almost any theatre. However, he goes on to offer a detailed description of how the theatre was transformed to an elegant ballroom with the whole so complete, and the metamorphosis accomplished in so short a time than any stranger who witnessed a performance on the Monday evening would scarcely credit that Tuesday's ball was conducted in the self same area.

The basic tale of each theatre's ups and downs, names and dates, financial capacity, etc, is peppered with anecdotes that build up a fascinating picture of backstage life, including the west country circuit actors who were generally called the Brandy Company from the intemperance of its members. At Tunbridge Wells, with its stage in Sussex and auditorium in Kent, the hand of justice could be be evaded. However, in other respects Winston took a poor view of this theatre – The dressing rooms which are under the stage are bad; and the green room, the actor's luxury, is to be erected when Mrs Manager shall think one necessary. The box office could not have been helped much by his rather scathing comment there are only two things necessary to render Tunbridge Wells an excellent theatre – good actors and good scenery: though, to confess the truth, the decorations are but scanty.

More Winston material is lurking in overseas libraries, particularly in Harvard and Sydney, and it is good to know that David Wilmore is researching the rest of the 283 theatres for which Winston made notes and sketches. Meanwhile I continue to enjoy my Lewes print – but with a much enhanced awareness of its context.

[ISBN 978 0 7123 5015 O]

Fragments of Wilderness City
– The work of Bryan Avery (2011)

This is an essential read for anyone seriously interested in architecture in general and performances spaces in particular. Although a record of the work of Bryan Avery, it is much more than that. With Avery but one of the six authors – the others are eminent architectural professionals but not members of the Avery Associates practice – this book provides a rare insight into the workings of the architectural mind. An analysis by Richard Weston of the buildings that influenced Avery is followed by a brilliant essay by the architect himself on the development of cities in which he gives the clearest exposition of environmental disintegration that I have encountered and offers solutions with a true ring of viability. That this is not just all pipe dreams is illustrated by Joseph Rykwert's chapter on Avery's urban projects, realised and unrealised.

Discussions on the workplace and innovation by John Worthington and Matthew Teague lead naturally to a commentary on performance spaces. For me, his RADA is the summit of the courtyard format and my enthusiasm is well documented. The Jerwood Vanbrugh takes cross auditorium focused side seating as far as it can go. The next step surely is to find a way of enabling side seated audience to see the stage without trunk twisting or neck craning. It may be a case of looking back at the likes of Gelsenkirchen and Inverness to move forward. Wexford is well on the way but will someone please commission a 600 seater from Bryan Avery. If in any doubt, read Edwin Heathcote's chapter on The Cultural Dimension.

Avery's other essay voices a concern that the aesthetics of design have become concentrated on satisfying the mind rather than the eye. Suggesting that our minds are active but our eyes are closed, his brief discourse on the geometry of vision – a model of clarity – is a persuasive argument for the old saying Beauty is in the Eye of the Beholder being literally true.

A chronology of Bryan Avery's principal projects concludes the book, which is beautifully illustrated throughout – a pleasure for the eye to behold!

[ISBN 978 1 904772 58 3]

Three Royals in Theatre Street

The history of the three Royals that give Norwich's Theatre Street its name is a tale of rebuilds, refurbishments and rebrandings amidst the roller coaster of alternating highs and lows endemic in the world of performance. Fortunately, the record of these ups and downs in Norwich Theatre Royal – The First 250 Years by Michael and Carol Blackwell finds today's Theatre Royal riding high after a splendid makeover.

But the precarious nature of theatre survival is illustrated by an episode as recently as the 1980s when, within less than a decade, one of the country's most successful theatres descended into an extended closure with its flytower demolished and no money in place to rebuild it. The pages on the meteoric rise during the Dick Condon era and the subsequent collapse into bureaucratic quagmire are essential reading for students of arts management. Indeed the 33 appended references on this subject would provide a researcher with a good start point for a useful case study analysing Condon's marketing skills, his mesmeric influence on his audience, and the damage, still lingering today, inflicted by the doctrinaire fervour with which he attacked the concept of subsidy as a component of arts funding.

The first Theatre was built by Thomas Ivory in 1757 and granted Royal status in 1768 by Act of Parliament. The committee books of the early years provide a fascinating glimpse into some of the finer details of running a theatre that, by the end of the 18th century, was in dire need of refurbishment with a list of problems that would have regular resonances down through the ages. From this material and a combing of the local newspapers, the Blackwell's provide a detailed insight into Georgian theatregoing.

William Wilkins carried out an extensive renovation in 1805. Then his son, the Wilkins of the National Gallery and Bury St Edmunds, built a new theatre which lasted, with various alterations, until it burned down in 1934 to be replaced by a cine-variety house from standard off-the-shelf plans for generic Odeons. This is the Theatre Royal that, following three extensive revisionist refurbishments, stands today.

All this is detailed in the book's fascinating account of the Norwich stage, its actors and its audience. The story includes the impact on the Royal of the Grand Opera House, later Hippodrome, built in 1902 by Sprague, architect of such distinguished west end houses as the ones that my generation still think of as the Albery (or even as the New), Aldwych, Globe and Wyndhams. In 1966, the City Council owned both theatres but, with no Theatres Trust yet in place to advise and if necessary invoke statutory powers, the Sprague was demolished and the site suffered the ignominy of becoming the Hippodrome car park. After 40 years of working and seeing shows at the Royal, I have considerable affection for it. So I feel some disloyalty in wishing that if only one theatre could survive it should have been the Sprague.

But, cheer up Francis! Just up the road, to brighten your fading years, there is now a comfortable theatre, courtesy of Tim Foster who has worked wonders in transforming the inadequacies of the third Theatre Royal to earn a place alongside Ivory and Wilkins (father and son) in this 250 year history now so entertainingly documented by Michael and Carole Blackwell.

[ISBN 9780955745409]

Architect, Actor and Audience

It is significant that Iain Mackintosh has called his book Architecture, Actor and Audience rather than Architect, Actor and Audience: he clearly feels that theatre architecture is not something to be left in the hands of architects,

His book is written from the viewpoint of the theatre consultant, a young profession born out of necessity when the accepted notion of a theatre building, for so long stable from one generation to the next, suddenly exploded into a wide range of co-existing alternative forms. Paranoia is rife among architects and likely to be increased by this book, although not, I think, by the half dozen or so architects whom I might consider hiring if I had funds to build my own theatre. (I will happily reveal this shortlist to anyone who cares to sponsor a hod of bricks for the new Norwich Playhouse).

Over the last couple of decades, Iain Mackintosh has done for theatre architecture what Fred Bentham did earlier for theatre lighting: acted as a major catalyst. Unlike Fred, Iain has a habit of not saying what we expect to hear. Sometimes it is not what we would like to hear. But it is always said articulately and it always stimulates our thinking – even if, from time to time, his ideas induce not agreement but reaction, enabling us to see and adopt a clearer but different way forward. I have a hunch that, in future, such catalytic people are going to be even more important as the philosophy known as political correctness tightens its deadening grip on the arts.

Iain is at his best when he surrenders to his idealism, From time to time – perhaps more frequently in his life than in his writings – he remembers that he works for a large consultancy firm subject to market forces. The resultant pragmatism does not lie easily upon him but is fortunately transparent. In his book, Iain the idealist is in full flight: share his vision or your theatre will perish.

Nevertheless, on this occasion, his writing does seem surprisingly restrained. Perhaps it is the effect of publication in a series labelled 'Theatre Concepts' under an editor of such academic weight as John Russell Brown. Perhaps the restraint is because the book's purpose is not to offer a new burst of Mackintosh originality but to take stock of where theatre architecture currently stands and how it got to this point. Its stimulation target is not those of us who have spent much of our lives agonising over theatre form, but a wider readership who have not been party to the debate on a regular basis but now need to have it summarised. His review of where many post-war theatres went wrong is a tightly acute objective analysis. His account of the subsequent reaction against these less successful theatres is inevitably more subjective, because many of the newer ones were built either with his involvement or in accordance with his ideology. His view of the future is less clearly revealed, but he does offer a succinct summary of the acknowledged potholes along the way ahead.

Actors and audiences are great survivors. They regularly conspire together to make dramatic performances come alive in theatres which offer a poor supportive environment. Two particularly major factors affect the quality of theatre architecture: one has always been with us, while the other, although gathering some momentum in the final quarter of the 19th Century, only became dominant in the second half of the 20th. The age-old problem is the pressure to squeeze-in more and more audience – a pressure that is becoming increasingly intense with the privatisation of culture, even in Central European countries where a long tradition of public subsidy has hitherto permitted theatre capacities to be held at optimun levels. The newer problem is the lateral growth of theatre into an ever widening range of coexisting forms. Each theatre form has its dedicated bunch of supporters who lobby with doctrinaire zeal. Consequently, much 20th Century theatre building is the result of setting temporary fashions in permanent concrete.

As a result, the future may need rather clearer definition of the function of the various types of people who practice under the banner of theatre consultancy, Three areas of advice are required by clients and their architect: objective analysis of alternative possibilities, expertise in the specialist design aspects of a theatre, and expertise in the details of its technical furnishing.

It is interesting that Iain Macintosh now tends to act as, and indeed call himself, a theatre building designer rather than consultant. I would trust Iain Mackintosh to build me the kind of theatre he believes in. But, precisely because that is his forte, I doubt if I would be entirely happy to invite him to provide me with an objective analysis of all the available options.

And so it is with his Architecture, Actor and Audience. It is a very readable, entertaining collection of essays on aspects of theatre architecture examined from the user's viewpoint. Its particular strengths lie in such areas as its explanation of the nature of actor-audience interaction, its analysis of auditorium verticals and its eloquence for a return to a much wider differential between expensive and cheap seats. Its weakness is some reluctance to acknowledge the potential merit of alternative viewpoints.

Everyone who works in theatres or attends performances will find stimulation in the book. All the architects will read it. So will we happy band of theatre architecture fetishists. But the target audience must be actors and their audience. I have a hunch that, at worst, we theatre nuts are imposing our ideas on the audience without considering their preferences or, at best, giving them what is good for them without helping them to understand why. Here is a book that could help involve the audience in their own destiny.

[ISBN: 9780415031837]

Theatre Buildings: a design guide

Straight to the point – this book is a must have for everyone involved in the commissioning or the building of theatres and in the manufacturing, selling, specifying or use of stage technology. It is destined to become a, perhaps even the, key reference on our bookshelves.

The spine reads Theatre Buildings but the rest of the full title, A Design Guide, defines the book's purpose. It is a guide: it does not replace any of the specialists in the complex team whose interactions produce a fit for purpose building. The book has been written by a team of over 50 of these specialists and they write from the perspective of hands-on doing it rather than just studying it. That all these people, each of them passionate about theatre in general and their own area in particular, could produce a cohesive narrative is a tribute to the editorial skills of Judith Strong. To anyone doubting that a coalition can produce consensus under inspired leadership, this ABTT book provides a resounding "Oh yes it can!".

The chapters follow the process of designing a theatre: Preliminary Planning, Broad Principles, Front of House, Auditorium, the Stage and its Machinery, Lighting, Sound & Video, Backstage areas, and the accommodation for management plus the ancillary activities that have developed theatres from hosting only evening performances into open all hours centres for educational and community projects. With input from John Earl, his predecessor at the Theatres Trust, Peter Longman contributes a chapter on the restoration and improvement of existing theatres. The final section, occupying over a third of the pages, is devoted to 28 theatres, 19 in the UK and nine overseas, that illustrate many of the points made in the specialist subject chapters. All the selected theatres provide positive references of good practice. Crucially, all 55 plans and sections are drawn to the same scale and relate clearly to the photographs.

Written in traditional theatre language (I found only one use of my personal bete noire "back of house") this is an easy book to read. Concise and precise, it explains with remarkable clarity the circumstances, mandatory or optional, in which each item on the bullet-pointed lists should be considered. The approach is holistic and to maximise its value, the reader does really need to avoid the temptation to just head for their own specialist chapter. This is a book that both stimulates thinking and provides lists to check omissions in that thinking.

As the ABTT approaches its 50th birthday, Theatre Buildings A Design Guide is a timely reminder of how this association of those who support the actor has brought together architects, equipment manufacturers and users in a classic example of a whole being more than the sum of its parts. While its is a book for today and the immediate future, it will eventually, like its predecessors of 1972 and 1986, provide future historians with a wonderful snapshot of how we were.

[ISBN : 9780415548946]

7 AN OBITUARY

Ken Smalley

As Technical Officer of the ABTT throughout the late 60s and most of the 70s, Ken Smalley was a key pioneer in the development of technical theatre training. This was a period when the formal backstage courses offered by drama schools were based primarily on the acquisition of stage management skills. While these courses did include practical stage experience, they were not geared to meeting the crewing needs of a theatre that was on a fast-track absorption of new technologies. The Arts Council recognised the problem and provided the ABBT with funding to explore fresh possibilities for training and to develop sources of technical information.

Starting his career as a dancer with Ballet Rambert, Ken Smalley had wide experience as a technician before moving from the Mermaid Theatre to the ABTT where he rapidly became an invaluable information resource. We rang Ken then in the way that we google now. He developed a series of factual information cards on a wide range of technical topics. These were sent to members as monthly mailings of batches of A4 sheets to be cut into four filing cards that built up into a resource base of useful hardware and where to fmd it. The format was so useful that it was copied by the Bühnetechnsische Rundschau.

With these mailings came a newsletter that became known informally as the Smalley Times. This was a mix of newspaper and magazine cuttings with typewritten bits of news written by Ken and by members who he tended to ring on the eve of going to print. He badgered us a bit but we cooperated because the ABTT was at the cutting edge of exciting times.

He had an uncanny instinct for knowing who might have a news item or a controversial view and so the Smalley Times often peppered its facts with quite sharp debate. In the days before digital cut and paste, publication was laborious work with scalpel and glue pot followed by endless turning of a duplicator handle while getting spattered with ink in a tradition originating with Caxton and only recently lost. Ken's skill in press cutting was to cull not just technical items but the very wide context in which theatre technology operates. When the Arts Council withdrew support and we lost Ken, we also lost a potential webmaster who could have made our website the pivot of the ABTT.

Ken was a lateral thinker – perhaps a touch too lateral for some of his more staid colleagues – and he got things done. His daily swim and exercise regime gave him boundless energy and there was something metaphoric about his daily attire – a safari suit – as he set out to implement ABTT in-service training programmes. Using telephone conference calls, he was able to set up an informed debate about the direction and details of a way forward.

Two of Ken's achievements were, in my view, particularly notable. With Paddington Tech, he was pivotal in setting up the theatre electricians' course attended by many of today's leading resident and production electricians. And he developed a particularly effective 24 hour lighting design course formula based on productions running in regional reps.

Participants were sent an information pack with all available plans, lists and details of the production and the theatre. They were asked to bring a lighting design plan to an afternoon session where all the plans were shared and compared with a lighting designer as animateur. Only after this session did they go on stage to look at the set and unlit rig. After seeing the show and an extended discussion in the bar, next morning brought a flash out followed by a session with as a many of the production team as could be gathered together. When we had director and/or set designer with us, these debates were some of the most fruitful I have experienced.

Then, in one of its rather infamous priority shifts, the Arts Council abandoned the ABTT and we lost Ken Smalley. He became a Fellow in recognition of his achievements but rarely appeared at Association functions. His influence on the development of ABTT cannot be overstated.

ENTERTAINMENT TECHNOLOGY PRESS

FREE SUBSCRIPTION SERVICE

Keeping Up To Date with

A Theatric Miscellany

Entertainment Technology titles are continually up-dated, and all major changes and additions are listed in date order in the relevant dedicated area of the publisher's website. Simply go to the front page of www.etnow.com and click on the BOOKS button. From there you can locate the title and be connected through to the latest information and services related to the publication.

The author of the title welcomes comments and suggestions about the book and can be contacted by email at: francisreid@btinternet.com

Titles Published by Entertainment Technology Press

50 Rigging Calls *Chris Higgs, Cristiano Giavedoni 246pp* **£16.95**
ISBN: 9781904031758
Chris Higgs, author of ETP's two leading titles on rigging, An Introduction to Rigging in the Entertainment Industry and Rigging for Entertainment: Regulations and Practice, has collected together 50 articles he has provided regularly for Lighting + Sound International magazine from 2005 to date. They provide a wealth of information for those practising the craft within the entertainment technology industry. The book is profusely illustrated with caricature drawings by Christiano Giavedoni, featuring the popular rigging expert Mario.

ABC of Theatre Jargon *Francis Reid 106pp* **£9.95** ISBN: 9781904031093
This glossary of theatrical terminology explains the common words and phrases that are used in normal conversation between actors, directors, designers, technicians and managers.

Aluminium Structures in the Entertainment Industry *Peter Hind 234pp* **£24.95**
ISBN: 9781904031062
Aluminium Structures in the Entertainment Industry aims to educate the reader in all aspects of the design and safe usage of temporary and permanent aluminium structures specific to the entertainment industry – such as roof structures, PA towers, temporary staging, etc.

Autocad – A Handbook for Theatre Users *David Ripley 340pp* **£29.95**
ISBN: 9781904031741
From 'Setting Up' to 'Drawing in Three Dimensions' via 'Drawings Within Drawings', this compact and fully illustrated guide to AutoCAD covers everything from the basics to full colour rendering and remote 3D plotting. Third, completely revised edition, June 2014.

Automation in the Entertainment Industry – A User's Guide *Mark Ager and John Hastie 382pp* **£29.95** ISBN: 9781904031581
In the last 15 years, there has been a massive growth in the use of automation in entertainment, especially in theatres, and it is now recognised as its own discipline. However, it is still only used in around 5% of theatres worldwide. In the next 25 years, given current growth patterns, that figure will rise to 30%. This will mean that the majority of theatre personnel, including directors, designers, technical staff, actors and theatre management, will come into contact with automation for the first time at some point in their careers. This book is intended to provide insights and practical advice from those who use automation, to help the first-time user understand the issues and avoid the pitfalls in its implementation.

Basics – A Beginner's Guide to Lighting Design *Peter Coleman 92pp* **£9.95**
ISBN: 9781904031413
The fourth in the author's 'Basics' series, this title covers the subject area in four main sections: The Concept, Practical Matters, Related Issues and The Design Into Practice. In an area that is difficult to be definitive, there are several things that cross all the boundaries of all lighting design and it's these areas that the author seeks to help with.

Basics – A Beginner's Guide to Special Effects *Peter Coleman 82pp* **£9.95**
ISBN: 9781904031338
This title introduces newcomers to the world of special effects. It describes all types of special effects including pyrotechnic, smoke and lighting effects, projections, noise machines, etc. It places emphasis on the safe storage, handling and use of pyrotechnics.

Basics – A Beginner's Guide to Stage Lighting *Peter Coleman 86pp* **£9.95**
ISBN: 9781904031208
This title does what it says: it introduces newcomers to the world of stage lighting. It will not teach the reader the art of lighting design, but will teach beginners much about the 'nuts and bolts' of stage lighting.

Basics – A Beginner's Guide to Stage Sound *Peter Coleman 86pp* **£9.95**
ISBN: 9781904031277
This title does what it says: it introduces newcomers to the world of stage sound. It will not teach the reader the art of sound design, but will teach beginners much about the background to sound reproduction in a theatrical environment.

Basics: A Beginner's Guide to Stage Management *Peter Coleman 64pp* **£7.95**
ISBN: 9781904031475
The fifth in Peter Coleman's popular 'Basics' series, this title provides a practical insight into, and the definition of, the role of stage management. Further chapters describe Cueing or 'Calling' the Show (the Prompt Book), and the Hardware and Training for Stage Management. This is a book about people and systems, without which most of the technical equipment used by others in the performance workplace couldn't function.

Building Better Theaters *Michael Mell 180pp* **£16.95** ISBN: 9781904031406
A title within our Consultancy Series, this book describes the process of designing a theatre, from the initial decision to build through to opening night. Michael Mell's book provides a step-by-step guide to the design and construction of performing arts facilities. Chapters discuss: assembling your team, selecting an architect, different construction methods, the architectural design process, construction of the theatre, theatrical systems and equipment, the stage, backstage, the auditorium, ADA requirements and the lobby. Each chapter clearly describes what to expect and how to avoid surprises. It is a must-read for architects, planners, performing arts groups, educators and anyone who may be considering building or renovating a theatre.

Carry on Fading *Francis Reid 216pp* **£20.00** ISBN: 9781904031642
This is a record of five of the best years of the author's life. Years so good that the only downside is the pangs of guilt at enjoying such contentment in a world full of misery induced by greed, envy and imposed ideologies. Fortunately Francis' DNA is high on luck, optimism and blessing counting.

Case Studies in Crowd Management
Chris Kemp, Iain Hill, Mick Upton, Mark Hamilton 206pp **£16.95**
ISBN: 9781904031482
This important work has been compiled from a series of research projects carried out by
the staff of the Centre for Crowd Management and Security Studies at Buckinghamshire
Chilterns University College (now Bucks New University), and seminar work carried out
in Berlin and Groningen with partner Yourope. It includes case studies, reports and a crowd
management safety plan for a major outdoor rock concert, safe management of rock concerts
utilising a triple barrier safety system and pan-European Health & Safety Issues.

Case Studies in Crowd Management, Security and Business Continuity
Chris Kemp, Patrick Smith 274pp **£24.95** ISBN: 9781904031635
The creation of good case studies to support work in progress and to give answers to those
seeking guidance in their quest to come to terms with perennial questions is no easy task.
The first Case Studies in Crowd Management book focused mainly on a series of festivals
and events that had a number of issues which required solving. This book focuses on a
series of events that had major issues that impacted on the every day delivery of the events
researched.

Close Protection – The Softer Skills *Geoffrey Padgham 132pp* **£11.95**
ISBN: 9781904031390
This is the first educational book in a new 'Security Series' for Entertainment
Technology Press, and it coincides with the launch of the new 'Protective Security
Management' Foundation Degree at Buckinghamshire Chilterns University College
(now Bucks New University). The author is a former full-career Metropolitan Police
Inspector from New Scotland Yard with 27 years' experience of close protection (CP).
For 22 of those years he specialised in operations and senior management duties with
the Royalty Protection Department at Buckingham Palace, followed by five years
in the private security industry specialising in CP training design and delivery. His
wealth of protection experience comes across throughout the text, which incorporates
sound advice and exceptional practical guidance, subtly separating fact from fiction.
This publication is an excellent form of reference material for experienced operatives,
students and trainees.

A Comparative Study of Crowd Behaviour at Two Major Music Events
Chris Kemp, Iain Hill, Mick Upton 78pp **£7.95** ISBN: 9781904031253
A compilation of the findings of reports made at two major live music concerts, and in
particular crowd behaviour, which is followed from ingress to egress.

Control Freak *Wayne Howell 270pp* **£28.95** ISBN: 9781904031550
Control Freak is the second book by Wayne Howell. It provides an in depth study of
DMX512 and the new RDM (Remote Device Management) standards. The book is aimed
at both users and developers and provides a wealth of real world information based on the
author's twenty year experience of lighting control.

Copenhagen Opera House *Richard Brett and John Offord 272pp* **£32.00**
ISBN: 9781904031420
Completed in a little over three years, the Copenhagen Opera House opened with a royal gala performance on 15th January 2005. Built on a spacious brown-field site, the building is a landmark venue and this book provides the complete technical background story to an opera house set to become a benchmark for future design and planning. Sixteen chapters by relevant experts involved with the project cover everything from the planning of the auditorium and studio stage, the stage engineering, stage lighting and control and architectural lighting through to acoustic design and sound technology plus technical summaries.

Corporate Event Production – Effective, face-to-face, corporate communication or Reaching 'The guy at the back, with bad eyesight - who'd rather be in the bar' *David Clement 324pp* **£29.95** ISBN: 9781904031840
A real-world insight into a specific industry sector: Corporate Event Production – the business of face-to-face communication. What it actually feels like to work in live events. The subtitle of 'Reaching the guy at the back with bad eyesight – who'd rather be in the bar' encapsulates the producer's challenge of creating an equally memorable experience for all attendees.
Structured around the project timeline – from receipt of a brief, to creative response and pitching, through pre-production design and planning to creating and directing the show on the day – the book is full of industry anecdotes, over 160 reference images, useful tips and guidelines. The stage-by-stage process of designing an engaging and truly effective live event.

Cue 80 *Francis Reid 310pp* **£17.95** ISBN: 9781904031659
Although Francis Reid's work in theatre has been visual rather than verbal, writing has provided crucial support. Putting words on paper has been the way in which he organised and clarified his thoughts. And in his self-confessed absence of drawing skills, writing has helped him find words to communicate his visual thinking in discussions with the rest of the creative team. As a by-product, this process of searching for the right words to help formulate and analyse ideas has resulted in half-a-century of articles in theatre journals. Cue 80 is an anthology of these articles and is released in celebration of Francis' 80th birthday.

The DMX 512-A Handbook – Design and Implementation of DMX Enabled Products and Networks *James Eade 150pp* **£13.95** ISBN: 9781904031727
This guidebook was originally conceived as a guide to the new DMX512-A standard on behalf of the ESTA Controls Protocols Working Group (CPWG). It has subsequently been updated and is aimed at all levels of reader from technicians working with or servicing equipment in the field as well as manufacturers looking to build in DMX control to their lighting products. It also gives thorough guidance to consultants and designers looking to design DMX networks.

Electric Shadows: an Introduction to Video and Projection on Stage *Nick Moran 234pp*
£23.95 ISBN: 9781904031734
Electric Shadows aims to guide the emerging video designer through the many simple and difficult technical and aesthetic choices and decisions he or she has to make in taking their design from outline idea through to realisation. The main body of the book takes the reader through the process of deciding what content will be projected onto what screen or screens to make the best overall production design. The book will help you make electric shadows that capture the attention of your audience, to help you tell your stories in just the way you want.

Electrical Safety for Live Events *Marco van Beek 98pp* **£16.95** ISBN: 9781904031284
This title covers electrical safety regulations and good practise pertinent to the entertainment industries and includes some basic electrical theory as well as clarifying the "do's and don't's" of working with electricity.

Entertainment Electronics *Anton Woodward 154pp* **£15.95** ISBN: 9781904031819
Electronic engineering in theatres has become quite prevalent in recent years, whether for lighting, sound, automation or props – so it has become an increasingly important skill for the theatre technician to possess. This book is intended to give the theatre technician a good grasp of the fundamental principles of electronics without getting too bogged down with maths so that many of the mysteries of electronics are revealed.

Entertainment in Production Volume 1: 1994-1999 *Rob Halliday 254pp* **£24.95**
ISBN: 9781904031512
Entertainment in Production Volume 2: 2000-2006 *Rob Halliday 242poo* £24.95
ISBN: 9781904031529
Rob Halliday has a dual career as a lighting designer/programmer and author and in these two volumes he provides the intriguing but comprehensive technical background stories behind the major musical productions and other notable projects spanning the period 1994 to 2005. Having been closely involved with the majority of the events described, the author is able to present a first-hand and all-encompassing portrayal of how many of the major shows across the past decade came into being. From *Oliver!* and *Miss Saigon* to *Mamma Mia!* and *Mary Poppins*, here the complete technical story unfolds. The books, which are profusely illustrated, are in large part an adapted selection of articles that first appeared in the magazine *Lighting&Sound International*.

Entertainment Technology Yearbook 2008 *John Offord 220pp* **£14.95**
ISBN: 9781904031543
The Entertainment Technology Yearbook 2008 covers the year 2007 and includes picture coverage of major industry exhibitions in Europe compiled from the pages of Entertainment Technology magazine and the etnow.com website, plus articles and pictures of production, equipment and project highlights of the year.

The Exeter Theatre Fire *David Anderson 202pp* **£24.95** ISBN: 9781904031130
This title is a fascinating insight into the events that led up to the disaster at the Theatre Royal, Exeter, on the night of September 5th 1887. The book details what went wrong, and the lessons that were learned from the event.

Fading into Retirement *Francis Reid 124pp* **£17.95** ISBN: 9781904031352
This is the final book in Francis Reid's fading trilogy which, with Fading Light and Carry on Fading, updates the Hearing the Light record of places visited, performances seen, and people met. Never say never, but the author uses the 'final' label because decreasing mobility means that his ability to travel is diminished to the point that his life is now contained within a very few square miles. His memories are triggered by over 600 CDs, half of them Handel and 100 or so DVDs supplemented by a rental subscription to LOVEFiLM.

Fading Light – A Year in Retirement *Francis Reid 136pp* **£14.95**
ISBN: 9781904031352
Francis Reid, the lighting industry's favourite author, describes a full year in retirement. "Old age is much more fun than I expected," he says. Fading Light describes visits and experiences to the author's favourite theatres and opera houses, places of relaxation and re-visits to scholarly institutions.

Focus on Lighting Technology *Richard Cadena 120pp* **£17.95** ISBN: 9781904031147
This concise work unravels the mechanics behind modern performance lighting and appeals to designers and technicians alike. Packed with clear, easy-to-read diagrams, the book provides excellent explanations behind the technology of performance lighting.

The Followspot Guide *Nick Mobsby 450pp* **£28.95** ISBN: 9781904031499
The first in ETP's Equipment Series, Nick Mobsby's Followspot Guide tells you everything you need to know about followspots, from their history through to maintenance and usage. Its pages include a technical specification of 193 followspots from historical to the latest versions from major manufacturers.

From Ancient Rome to Rock 'n' Roll – a Review of the UK Leisure Security Industry
Mick Upton 198pp **£14.95** ISBN: 9781904031505
From stewarding, close protection and crowd management through to his engagement as a senior consultant Mick Upton has been ever present in the events industry. A founder of ShowSec International in 1982 he was its chairman until 2000. The author has led the way on training within the sector. He set up the ShowSec Training Centre and has acted as a consultant at the Bramshill Police College. He has been prominent in the development of courses at Buckinghamshire New University where he was awarded a Doctorate in 2005. Mick has received numerous industry awards. His book is a personal account of the development and professionalism of the sector across the past 50 years.

Gobos for Image Projection *Michael Hall and Julie Harper 176pp* **£25.95**
ISBN: 9781904031628
In this first published book dedicated totally to the gobo, the authors take the reader through from the history of projection to the development of the present day gobo. And there is broad practical advice and ample reference information to back it up. A feature of the work is the inclusion, interspersed throughout the text, of comment and personal experience in the use and application of gobos from over 25 leading lighting designers worldwide.

Health and Safety Aspects in the Live Music Industry *Chris Kemp, Iain Hill 300pp*
£30.00 ISBN: 9781904031222
This major work includes chapters on various safety aspects of live event production and is written by specialists in their particular areas of expertise.

Health and Safety in the Live Music and Event Technical Produciton Industry
Chris Hannam 74pp **£12.95** ISBN: 9781904031802
This book covers the real basics of health and safety in the live music and event production industry in a simple jargon free manner that can also be used as the perfect student course note accompaniment to the various safety passport schemes that now exist in our industry.

Health and Safety Management for Tour and Production Managers and
Self-Employment in the Live Music and Events Industry
Chris Hannam 136pp **£11.95** ISBN: 9781904031864
Two books in one: **Health and Safety Management for Tour and Production Managers** is designed to give simple, basic health and safety information to bands, artists, tour, stage and production managers, crew chiefs, heads of department, supervisors or line managers and has been designed as a follow on from *Health And Safety in the Live Music and Event Technical Production Industry*. It will also be of use to local crew companies, especially their crew chiefs and managers.
The second book is **Self-Employment in the Live Music and Events Industry**
A Guide for the Self-Employed and those who use the services of the Self-Employed

Health and Safety Management in the Live Music and Events Industry *Chris Hannam*
480pp **£25.95** ISBN: 9781904031307
This title covers the health and safety regulations and their application regarding all aspects of staging live entertainment events, and is an invaluable manual for production managers and event organisers.

Hearing the Light – 50 Years Backstage *Francis Reid 280pp* **£24.95**
ISBN: 9781904031185
This highly enjoyable memoir delves deeply into the theatricality of the industry. The author's almost fanatical interest in opera, his formative period as lighting designer at Glyndebourne and his experiences as a theatre administrator, writer and teacher make for a broad and unique background.

Introduction to Live Sound *Roland Higham 174pp* **£16.95**
ISBN: 9781904031796
This new title aims to provide working engineers and newcomers alike with a concise knowledge base that explains some of the theory and principles that they will encounter every day. It should provide for the student and newcomer to the field a valuable compendium of helpful knowledge.

An Introduction to Rigging in the Entertainment Industry *Chris Higgs 272pp* **£24.95**
ISBN: 9781904031123
This title is a practical guide to rigging techniques and practices and also thoroughly covers
safety issues and discusses the implications of working within recommended guidelines and
regulations. Second edition revised September 2008.

Let There be Light – Entertainment Lighting Software Pioneers in Conversation
Robert Bell 390pp **£32.00** ISBN: 9781904031246
Robert Bell interviews a distinguished group of software engineers working on
entertainment lighting ideas and products.
Light and Colour Filters *Michael Hall and Eddie Ruffell 286pp* **£23.95**
ISBN: 9781904031598
Written by two acknowledged and respected experts in the field, this book is destined to
become the standard reference work on the subject. The title chronicles the development
and use of colour filters and also describes how colour is perceived and how filters function.
Up-to-date reference tables will help the practitioner make better and more specific choices
of colour.

Lighting for Roméo and Juliette *John Offord 172pp* **£26.95** ISBN: 9781904031161
John Offord describes the making of the Vienna State Opera production from the lighting
designer's viewpoint – from the point where director Jürgen Flimm made his decision not to
use scenery or sets and simply employ the expertise of lighting designer Patrick Woodroffe.

Lighting Systems for TV Studios *Nick Mobsby 570pp* **£45.00** ISBN: 9781904031000
Lighting Systems for TV Studios, now in its second edition, is the first book specifically
written on the subject and has become the 'standard' resource work for studio planning
and design covering the key elements of system design, luminaires, dimming, control,
data networks and suspension systems as well as detailing the infrastructure items such as
cyclorama, electrical and ventilation. TV lighting principles are explained and some history
on TV broadcasting, camera technology and the equipment is provided to help set the scene!
The second edition includes applications for sine wave and distributed dimming, moving
lights, Ethernet and new cool lamp technology.

Lighting Techniques for Theatre-in-the-Round *Jackie Staines 188pp* **£24.95**
ISBN: 9781904031017
Lighting Techniques for Theatre-in-the-Round is a unique reference source for those
working on lighting design for theatre-in-the-round for the first time. It is the first title to be
published specifically on the subject and it also provides some anecdotes and ideas for more
challenging shows, and attempts to blow away some of the myths surrounding lighting in
this format.

Lighting the Diamond Jubilee Concert *Durham Marenghi 102pp* **£19.95**
ISBN: 9781904031673
In this highly personal landmark document the show's lighting designer Durham Marenghi
pays tribute to the team of industry experts who each played an important role in bringing

the Diamond Jubilee Concert to fruition, both for television and live audiences. The book contains colour production photography throughout and describes the production processes and the thinking behind them. In his Foreword, BBC Executive Producer Guy Freeman states: "Working with the whole lighting team on such a special project was a real treat for me and a fantastic achievement for them, which the pages of this book give a remarkable insight into."

Lighting the Stage *Francis Reid 120pp* **£14.95** ISBN: 9781904031086
Lighting the Stage discusses the human relationships involved in lighting design – both between people, and between these people and technology. The book is written from a highly personal viewpoint and its 'thinking aloud' approach is one that Francis Reid has used in his writings over the past 30 years.

Miscellany of Lighting and Stagecraft *Michael Hall & Julie Harper 222pp* **£22.95** ISBN: 9781904031680
This title will help schools, colleges, amateurs, technicians and all those interested in practical theatre and performance to understand, in an entertaining and informative way, the key backstage skills. Within its pages, numerous professionals share their own special knowledge and expertise, interspersed with diversions of historic interest and anecdotes from those practising at the front line of the industry. As a result, much of the advice and skills set out have not previously been set in print. The editors' intention with this book is to provide a Miscellany that is not ordered or categorised in strict fashion, but rather encourages the reader to flick through or dip into it, finding nuggets of information and anecdotes to entertain, inspire and engender curiosity – also to invite further research or exploration and generally encourage people to enter the industry and find out for themselves.

Mr Phipps' Theatre *Mark Jones, John Pick 172pp* £17.95 ISBN: 9781904031383
Mark Jones and John Pick describe "The Sensational Story of Eastbourne's Royal Hippodrome" – formerly Eastbourne Theatre Royal. An intriguing narrative, the book sets the story against a unique social history of the town. Peter Longman, former director of The Theatres Trust, provides the Foreword.

Northen Lights *Michael Northen 256pp* **£17.95** ISBN: 9781904031666
Many books have been written by famous personalities in the theatre about their lives and work. However this is probably one of the first memoirs by someone who has spent his entire career behind scenes, and not in front of the footlights. As a lighting designer and as consultant to designers and directors, Michael Northen worked through an exciting period of fifty years of theatrical history from the late nineteen thirties in theatres in the UK and abroad, and on productions ranging from Shakespeare, opera and ballet to straight plays, pantomimes and cabaret. This is not a complicated technical text book, but is intended to give an insight into some of the 300 productions in which he had been involved and some of the directors, the designers and backstage staff he have worked with, viewed from a new angle.

Pages From Stages *Anthony Field 204pp* **£17.95** ISBN: 9781904031260
Anthony Field explores the changing style of theatres including interior design, exterior design, ticket and seat prices, and levels of service, while questioning whether the theatre still exists as a place of entertainment for regular theatre-goers.

People, Places, Performances *Remembered by Francis Reid 60pp* **£8.95** ISBN: 9781904031765
In growing older, the Author has found that memories, rather than featuring the events, increasingly tend to focus on the people who caused them, the places where they happened and the performances that arose. So Francis Reid has used these categories in endeavouring to compile a brief history of the second half of the twentieth century.

Performing Arts Technical Training Handbook 2013/2014 *ed: John Offord 304pp* **£19.95** ISBN: 9781904031710
Published in association with the ABTT (Association of British Theatre Technicians), this important Handbook, now in its third edition, includes fully detailed and indexed entries describing courses on backstage crafts offered by over 100 universities and colleges across the UK. A completely new research project, with accompanying website, the title also includes articles with advice for those considering a career 'behind the scenes', together with contact information and descriptions of the major organisations involved with industry training – plus details of companies offering training within their own premises.

Practical Dimming *Nick Mobsby 364pp* **£22.95** ISBN: 97819040313444
This important and easy to read title covers the history of electrical and electronic dimming, how dimmers work, current dimmer types from around the world, planning of a dimming system, looking at new sine wave dimming technology and distributed dimming. Integration of dimming into different performance venues as well as the necessary supporting electrical systems are fully detailed. Significant levels of information are provided on the many different forms and costs of potential solutions as well as how to plan specific solutions. Architectural dimming for the likes of hotels, museums and shopping centres is included. Practical Dimming is a companion book to Practical DMX and is designed for all involved in the use, operation and design of dimming systems.

Practical DMX *Nick Mobsby 276pp* **£16.95** ISBN: 9781904031369
In this highly topical and important title the author details the principles of DMX, how to plan a network, how to choose equipment and cables, with data on products from around the world, and how to install DMX networks for shows and on a permanently installed basis. The easy style of the book and the helpful fault finding tips, together with a review of different DMX testing devices provide an ideal companion for all lighting technicians and system designers. An introduction to Ethernet and Canbus networks are provided as well as tips on analogue networks and protocol conversion. It also includes a chapter on Remote Device Management.

A Practical Guide to Health and Safety in the Entertainment Industry
Marco van Beek 120pp **£14.95** ISBN: 9781904031048
This book is designed to provide a practical approach to Health and Safety within the Live Entertainment and Event industry. It gives industry-pertinent examples, and seeks to break down the myths surrounding Health and Safety.

Production Management *Joe Aveline 134pp* **£17.95** ISBN: 9781904031109
Joe Aveline's book is an in-depth guide to the role of the Production Manager, and includes real-life practical examples and 'Aveline's Fables' – anecdotes of his experiences with real messages behind them.

Rigging for Entertainment: Regulations and Practice *Chris Higgs 156pp* **£19.95** ISBN: 9781904031215
Continuing where he left off with his highly successful An Introduction to Rigging in the Entertainment Industry, Chris Higgs' second title covers the regulations and use of equipment in greater detail.

Rock Solid Ethernet *Wayne Howell 304pp* **£23.95** ISBN: 9781904031697
Now in its third completely revised and reset edition, Rock Solid Ethernet is aimed specifically at specifiers, installers and users of entertainment industry systems, and will give the reader a thorough grounding in all aspects of computer networks, whatever industry they may work in. The inclusion of historical and technical 'sidebars' make for an enjoyable as well as an informative read.

Sixty Years of Light Work *Fred Bentham 450pp* **£26.95** ISBN: 9781904031079
This title is an autobiography of one of the great names behind the development of modern stage lighting equipment and techniques. It includes a complete facsimile of the famous Strand Electric Catalogue of May 1936 – a reference work in itself.

Sound for the Stage *Patrick Finelli 218pp* **£24.95** ISBN: 9781904031154
Patrick Finelli's thorough manual covering all aspects of live and recorded sound for performance is a complete training course for anyone interested in working in the field of stage sound, and is a must for any student of sound.

Stage Automation *Anton Woodward 128pp* **£12.95** ISBN: 9781904031567
The purpose of this book is to explain the stage automation techniques used in modern theatre to achieve some of the spectacular visual effects seen in recent years. The book is targeted at automation operators, production managers, theatre technicians, stage engineering machinery manufacturers and theatre engineering students. Topics are covered in sufficient detail to provide an insight into the thought processes that the stage automation engineer has to consider when designing a control system to control stage machinery in a modern theatre. The author has worked on many stage automation projects and developed the award-winning Impressario stage automation system.

Stage Lighting Design in Britain: The Emergence of the Lighting Designer, 1881-1950
Nigel Morgan 300pp **£17.95** ISBN: 9781904031345
This title sets out to ascertain the main course of events and the controlling factors that determined the emergence of the theatre lighting designer in Britain, starting with the introduction of incandescent electric light to the stage, and ending at the time of the first public lighting design credits around 1950. The book explores the practitioners, equipment, installations and techniques of lighting design.

Stage Lighting for Theatre Designers *Nigel Morgan 124pp* **£17.95**
ISBN: 9781904031192
This is an updated second edition of Nigel Morgan's popular book for students of theatre design – outlining all the techniques of stage lighting design.

Technical Marketing – Ideas for Engineers *David Brooks. 376pp* **£26.95**
ISBN: 9781904031857
When *Technical Marketing Techniques* was published in 2000, marketing was poised on the threshold of a new era. What advertising and design agencies then termed 'new media' was merely a glimpse of what was to follow as the Internet came to dominate and transform the way we did things. We coined the term Technical Marketing to describe a new way of operating for businesses and how they marketed their products and services on a global platform. 'Technical Marketing – Ideas for Engineers' retains a major opening section covering traditional marketing theory and then in the second section demonstrates how online and offline techniques can be integrated into an effective marketing communications plan. The final section of the book reviews the still evolving possibilities of digital marketing which is beginning to re write the rules of marketing.

Technical Standards for Places of Entertainment (2015) *ABTT 366pp A4* **£60.00**
ISBN: 9781904031833
Technical Standards for Places of Entertainment details the necessary physical standards required for entertainment venues. Known in the industry as the "Yellow Book" the latest completely revised edition was first published in June 2015.

Theatre Engineering and Stage Machinery *Toshiro Ogawa 332pp* **£30.00**
ISBN: 9781904031024
Theatre Engineering and Stage Machinery is a unique reference work covering every aspect of theatrical machinery and stage technology in global terms, and across the complete historical spectrum. Revised February 2007.

Theatre Lighting in the Age of Gas *Terence Rees 232pp* **£24.95**
ISBN: 9781904031178
Entertainment Technology Press has republished this valuable historic work previously produced by the Society for Theatre Research in 1978. Theatre Lighting in the Age of Gas investigates the technological and artistic achievements of theatre lighting engineers from the 1700s to the late Victorian period.

Theatre Space: A Rediscovery Reported   *Francis Reid   238pp*   **£19.95**
ISBN: 9781904031437
In the post-war world of the 1950s and 60s, the format of theatre space became a matter for
a debate that aroused passions of an intensity unknown before or since. The proscenium
arch was clearly identified as the enemy, accused of forming a barrier to disrupt the relations
between the actor and audience. An uneasy fellow-traveller at the time, Francis Reid later
recorded his impressions whilst enjoying performances or working in theatres old and new
and this book is an important collection of his writings in various theatrical journals from
1969-2001 including his contribution to the Cambridge Guide to the Theatre in 1988. It
reports some of the flavour of the period when theatre architecture was rediscovering its past
in a search to establish its future.

The Theatres and Concert Halls of Fellner and Helmer   *Michael Sell   246pp*   **£23.95**
ISBN: 9781904031772
This is the first British study of the works of the prolific Fellner and Helmer Atelier which
was active from 1871-1914 during which time they produced over 80 theatre designs and
are second in quantity only to Frank Matcham, to whom reference is made.
This period is one of great change as a number of serious theatre fires which included
Nice and Vienna had the effect of the introduction of safety legislation which affected
theatre design. This study seeks to show how Fellner and Helmer and Frank Matcham
dealt with this increasing safety legislation, in particular the way in which safety was built
into their new three part theatres equipped with iron stages, safety curtains, electricity and
appropriate access and egress and, in the Vienna practice, how this was achieved across 13
countries.

Theatres of Achievement   *John Higgins   302pp*   **£29.95**   ISBN: 9781904031376
John Higgins affectionately describes the history of 40 distinguished UK theatres in a
personal tribute, each uniquely illustrated by the author. Completing each profile is colour
photography by Adrian Eggleston.

A Theatric Miscellany   *Francis Reid   154pp*   **£15.95**   ISBN: 9781904031871
This book is about memories. Some of them are highlights of the author's life. Recall of
other, more routine events, is triggered by discovery of a cache of sundry articles. A few
make predictions that are still relevant but most guess the future wrongly. Either way, they
make a small contribution to history.

Theatric Tourist   *Francis Reid   220pp*   **£19.95**   ISBN: 9781904031468
Theatric Tourist is the delightful story of Francis Reid's visits across more than 50 years
to theatres, theatre museums, performances and even movie theme parks. In his inimitable
style, the author involves the reader within a personal experience of venues from the Legacy
of Rome to theatres of the Renaissance and Eighteenth Century Baroque and the Gustavian
Theatres of Stockholm. His performance experiences include Wagner in Beyreuth, the
Pleasures of Tivoli and Wayang in Singapore. This is a 'must have' title for those who are as
"incurably stagestruck" as the author.

Through the Viewfinder *Jeremy Hoare 276pp* **£21.95** ISBN:: 9781904031574
Do you want to be a top television cameraman? Well this is going to help!
Through the Viewfinder is aimed at media students wanting to be top professional television cameramen – but it will also be of interest to anyone who wants to know what goes on behind the cameras that bring so much into our homes.
The author takes his own opinionated look at how to operate a television camera based on 23 years' experience looking through many viewfinders for a major ITV network company. Based on interviews with people he has worked with, all leaders in the profession, the book is based on their views and opinions and is a highly revealing portrait of what happens behind the scenes in television production from a cameraman's point of view.

Vectorworks for Theatre *Steve Macluskie 232pp* **£23.95** ISBN: 9781904031826
An essential reference manual for anyone using Vectorworks in the Theatre Industry. This book covers everything from introducing the basic tools to creating 3D design concepts and using worksheets to calculate stock usage and lighting design paperwork. A highly visual style using hundreds of high resolution screen images makes this a very easy book to follow whether novice or experienced user.

Walt Disney Concert Hall – The Backstage Story *Patricia MacKay & Richard Pilbrow 250pp* **£28.95** ISBN: 9781904031239
Spanning the 16-year history of the design and construction of the Walt Disney Concert Hall, this book provides a fresh and detailed behind the scenes story of the design and technology from a variety of viewpoints. This is the first book to reveal the "process" of the design of a concert hall.

Yesterday's Lights – A Revolution Reported *Francis Reid 352pp* **£26.95** ISBN: 9781904031321
Set to help new generations to be aware of where the art and science of theatre lighting is coming from – and stimulate a nostalgia trip for those who lived through the period, Francis Reid's latest book has over 350 pages dedicated to the task, covering the 'revolution' from the fifties through to the present day. Although this is a highly personal account of the development of lighting design and technology and he admits that there are 'gaps', you'd be hard put to find anything of significance missing.

Go to www.etbooks.co.uk for full details of above titles and secure online ordering facilities. Most books also available for Kindle.